CW01239065

The Cara Files
File 4: Lost

Copyright

Author: Tony Warner
Title: The Cara Files - File 4: Lost
A novella
© 2024, Tony Warner
Self-published
(Contact: psiwarbook@gmail.com)

All rights reserved.
No part of this publication may be reproduced, stored in a retrieval system, stored in a database and / or published in any form or by any means, electronic, mechanical, photocopying, recording or otherwise, without the prior written permission of the author.

Introduction

This novella is the fourth book in the Cara Files series. If you haven't read the first book: File 1 – The Chase, File 2 – Automata, and File 3 – Starship, I strongly recommend that you do so before reading this book.

The Cara Files: File 4 – Lost continues Cara's quest to be with Mei Xing. After surviving the perils of the Empty World, the Machine World, and the Starship, Cara now finds herself in yet another new universe.

Acknowledgments

Special thanks go to my wife who helped with the editing of this book. Thank you Sue.

Tony

Chapter 1

Cara was thoroughly miserable as she contemplated her last cigarette. Should she smoke it now? Or save it for later?

What's the difference? She thought to herself. Sighing, she lit it and drew in a lungful of smoke before letting it out in one big plume. Sometimes she wondered how she had ended up in this mess, lost in an unknown world in an unknown universe. Just the thought of it boggled the mind and although she was determined to continue her travels to be with Mei Xing, sometimes she missed her life and parents back in her world. Her relationship with her parents had always been distant. She assumed that was because she was different and didn't conform to societal norms. There was no boyfriend, no engagement, and no wedding. They didn't understand, couldn't understand, and probably never would. An invisible barrier existed between them, unspoken yet ever-present, keeping them apart. So she didn't miss them that much, but right now her flat in London with its comfortable bed and ensuite shower was exactly what she craved.

Sitting on the ground, just in the tree line, on the beach, she surveyed her tanned legs. Tiny bite marks and lumps covered her legs, the result of sleeping on the sand four nights ago. She assumed that there was some sort of sand mite analogue that lived in this world. Whatever they were, they liked to feast on her blood, and they itched like hell. As a result, she now spent her nights under the trees close to the beach. Venturing deeper into the forest proved impossible. It was incredibly dense, and, in any case, she wasn't sure what lived in its dark depths. One thing was for sure, there were definitely animals in there. Walking along the beach every day, desperate to find some sign of civilisation, she regularly heard squeaks, roars and shrieks made by numerous unseen creatures deep in that dark forest.

Her shorts were filthy, and her T-shirt ripped across the front, exposing her bra and too much skin. She didn't care, there was no one here to see it. She was alone. Alone and lost.

Six days ago, she had stepped through a portal in the Nandae world to arrive here. But somehow, her companions, Cheryl and Arx, were not with her. Had they somehow ended up in a different world? Even though they had all come through the same portal at the same time? Was that even possible? Or were they somewhere in this world? Lost, just as she was?

She took another drag from her cigarette, savouring the taste.

For six days she had been walking along the shoreline, hoping to meet someone, or find something, some tiny sign that there was a civilisation here, in this unknown and empty world. But there was nothing. There were only the trees, the ocean, the birds screeching in the sky, the hidden animals in the forest, and insects. There was no one here. She was on her own. She was well and truly lost.

She was hungry. Her little camp stove had run out of gas three days ago. After which she had scavenged some berries and fruit. She grimaced at the thought of the yellow fruit she had found. While it had tasted wonderful, it had not agreed with her at all. After eating it, she had promptly thrown it all back up. After which she felt very weak and unsteady and had to rest for an hour or so. Later, she had cleaned herself up in the ocean.

She considered herself lucky. The fruit could have been poisonous, possibly was poisonous. She could have died.

Since then, she was more careful, but she knew she needed more than just fruit and berries. She needed protein. So reluctantly, for the very first time, she had used the bracelet that Kate had given her. Pressing the hidden stud underneath the blue jewel, she had selected OFFENCE from the menu that appeared in her mind. The result had been shocking. Everything in a five-metre radius around her had died. All the plants, bushes and grass had turned brown, their leaves and fronds curling up as though burnt. Insects and leaves rained down on her from the trees above as they fell, quite dead. Even the trees themselves couldn't escape. They withered and twisted in upon themselves, their bark cracking and branches breaking. Dead things rained down on her, and a large object hitting the ground beside her made her jump. It was a large lizard type creature, some two metres in length. It too was dead.

The destructive power of the bracelet was frightening, but also reassuring. If a large animal threatened her, she could handle it.

She had never gutted an animal before. She had no idea what to do. So she experimented until she found a way that worked. She cut open its abdomen and pulled out all the organs. Once washed in the sea, she impaled it on a sharp stick and held it over a fire. She figured it would be okay to eat as long as it was very well done. Sure enough, the blackened meat was delicious, and she had eaten her fill.

She sucked in another lungful of smoke and absently rubbed at her left forearm with her metal hand. It was covered in a rash which was red and swollen. Blowing out the smoke, she tipped her right foot up so she could look at the sole of her boot. It was loose and flapping. She would have to do something about that.

For six days she had held onto hope, but now it was gone. She would never find any evidence of people. She would never find Arx or Cheryl. Like her, they were lost forever.

Across the still ocean, in the far distance, Cara watched impassively as a new giant mushroom cloud billowed upwards. After a couple of minutes, the ground shook, causing leaves to fall from the trees above her, while bushes and grasses swayed. A long, low, deep rumbling, sounding like thunder, vibrated through her body. This was not the first time she had witnessed such an explosion. It had been happening every day since she had been in this world. Sometimes there was more than one. Once, she had witnessed three. It was fortunate that they were so far away and all that she saw was the mushroom cloud and orange flashes of flame within. She assumed they were nuclear. At least they looked like atomic explosions she had seen in documentaries and films on TV.

She wondered absently, why and how the explosions were being set off. Surely, they should affect the weather, wouldn't they? Why were there no winds streaming from the detonations, blowing dust, soil, water and God knows what across the ocean? It made no sense. Over there, the blasts were surely causing untold damage, yet over here, on this endless beach, it was calm and tranquil.

God knows how much radiation she had absorbed, but she was past caring. It was just one more thing she had to put up with.

The only thing that kept her going was Mei Xing. At least she could still contact her, even though she lived in some distant parallel universe.

'Keep going Cara,' Mei told her every day. *'You never know what's behind that bend or over that hill.'*

Latterly, Cara had become very negative about her situation.

'It's a waste of time, Mei,' she had told her. *'There's no one here but me. I'm lost.'*

'Something good will happen soon,' replied Mei. *'It has too. Don't give up!'* she implored.

'I don't know what to do,' said Cara miserably. *'I can't keep going on like this. Maybe this is the end.'*

'DON'T!' shouted Mei Xing. *'Don't you dare say that. Don't you dare give up on me! You will keep going and you will find help.'*

'There's no help to be found, Mei,' replied a morose Cara.

'There is, there has to be,' replied Mei vehemently. *'Don't you dare give up, or I'll never forgive you!'*

There had been many conversations like this. Mei doing her best to keep Cara's hopes alive, while Cara felt like giving up. She had never felt so miserable in her life.

She finished the cigarette. Cara sighed heavily and threw the butt to the ground. No more cigarettes, no more camp stove, no more food, no clean clothes and a lighter that would surely give up soon. Once it did, she would have to find a new way of lighting a fire. She was sure that wouldn't be easy.

Of course, it was her own fault, really. She had insisted that they travel through the middle portal of the three, back on the Nandae world. It was she who had made the decision to make the journey, even though there was no way of knowing where they would end up. No way of knowing which universe they would travel to. What she hadn't expected was that she would be alone.

Cara unlaced her boots and pulled them off. Unrolling her sleeping bag, she zipped herself inside and lay still, waiting for the dark of night to descend.

She sent out a desperate thought to Mei Xing.

'Mei, help me, please.'

As she slept, Cara was unaware of the machine managed processes happening inside her body. Unknown to her, the semi-organic device implanted at the base of her spine activated. Its sole purpose was to monitor and support all of Cara's biological systems, regulating hormone levels and producing billions of nanobots. The microscopic machines coursed through her bloodstream, maintaining organ structures and repairing damaged cells. As she rested, the nanobots provided her organs and cells with necessary nutrients, while eliminating toxins and pathogens.

The device kept her body functioning at peak efficiency. Little did she know that in the six days she had been in this world, she had walked two hundred and forty miles, a feat totally impossible without the support of the implanted device.

Without it, she would be dead.

———

The next morning was like every other morning, cold and miserable. Lying on her side in her sleeping bag, Cara watched the rolling waves crash onto the shore. It was always the same view. The endless beach, stretching from one horizon on her left and right. The deep, azure blue cloudless sky above, with the deep and dark forest behind her and the vast blue-green ocean that met the sky countless miles away.

There was no sign of movement apart from the waves breaking on the shore, and strange four-winged birds that sailed high in the sky, over the sea, their screeching cries sounding like metal grinding against metal.

She sighed. Today would be the same as every other day. The never-ending walking and the never changing scenery. Was there any point? What could she hope to achieve? As the days passed, it was becoming more and more obvious that no one lived here. This was another empty world, just like the world that she had first entered when she had begun her journey to be with Mei Xing. Was there any point carrying on walking? She would never find anyone.

But Mei insisted she kept going. Without her, she might have given up days ago. She trusted Mei. She loved her. It made her heart ache, knowing that she was so far away, so unreachable. She longed to be with her, to hold her, to love her. She regularly thought back to the time on the Starship, how she used to visit the Hibernation room to gaze at the duplicates of both her and Mei asleep in their suspension chamber. It was the first time that she had seen Mei in the flesh, and she was more beautiful than she had thought possible. Seeing the two of them, herself and Mei with their arms wrapped around each other, nearly broke her heart. Why couldn't she and her Mei be together like that? It wasn't fair.

Anger grew in her. She and Mei were destined to be together. It wasn't right that they were apart, they should be together. Her fingers curled into fists and her lips thinned. She had to find Mei. She just had to. The anger changed to resolve. She would be with Mei. She would do everything she could to ensure that happened.

Her emotional rollercoaster had travelled from the low of despair to the high of determination and hope. Ignorant of the device at the base of her spine, Cara had no knowledge of the subtle control it was exerting over her. Its rudimentary intelligence recognised Cara's emotional state and understood how it affected her wellbeing, prompting it to act by secreting dopamine, endorphins and serotonin - feel good hormones to help boost her mood. It was just one more way that the device tirelessly kept Cara functioning at her best, like a loyal guardian looking after its charge.

Skipping breakfast, Cara hastily gathered her few belongings and dropped them into her backpack on top of the lifeless cuboid machine she had named Mr Mapper. She had carried the small machine with her through the Nandae portal and into this world, and never once did she consider leaving it behind. Despite its non-functioning state, Cara clung to the possibility of somehow getting it repaired. Knowing that Mr Mapper possessed the ability to open portals between worlds, if she could get it fixed, she could escape this world. Though the chances of this were slim to nothing, it was the last piece of hope that she desperately clung to.

She trudged along the beach for four hours before stopping to use her bracelet once more to kill something to cook and eat. This time, a six-legged furry animal fell out of a tree. It was about the size of a squirrel and proved to be a challenge to skin and gut, but hunger drove her on. Soon the meat was sizzling over a roaring fire and after a few more minutes, she was cramming her mouth full of blackened, hot flesh.

As she ate, she gazed at the sea that went on for miles before it met the sky. As usual, everything was as it always was, until something caught her eye. Something flashed in the water, rolling back and forth as the waves gently broke onto the beach. This was the first time that she had seen anything other than the sea, beach and forest, and she was immediately excited to find out what it was.

She carefully placed the crispy meat on a stone nearby and stood, lifting the rim of her cap to allow a better view. There was definitely something flashing with the reflected sunlight in the breakwater. What was it? Was it artificial? Or was it some sort of creature that inhabited this world? Undoubtedly, there were lots of creatures that she had not yet seen, and although the sea had always been calm since she had arrived in this world, who knew what lived beneath the surface? It could be something with a silver or reflective carapace.

There was only one way to find out.

Over the last few weeks, Cara had travelled to many worlds and on some of them had come close to death. So she approached the object cautiously, half expecting it to leap up out of the water to attack her. As she drew closer, she saw the foaming turquoise water crashing over the smooth surface of a silver sphere, the gentle waves pushing it back and forth along the warm sand.

'Arx!' Cara screamed in delight, running into the water. Sinking to her knees, she reached out to grasp the silver orb.

As soon as she contacted its metal surface, an electric shock ripped through her. Immediately, she collapsed face down into the water, her body convulsing with violent spasms, her back arched and fingers curled inwards. An animal grunt escaped her lips, the water around her churning and bubbling as she struggled for breath.

In seconds, she was unconscious.

Chapter 2

Fortunately for Cara, the device implanted at the base of her spine came to her rescue once more. Its semi-organic intelligence detected the dangerous surge of electricity coursing through her body. Emergency safety protocols kicked in, deflecting the flow away from major organs and important neural pathways. It prevented spasming muscles from breaking sinews, and the energy flow from burning skin and boiling fluids by channelling it away into the pervasive dark energy field. After inducing unconsciousness, the device manipulated muscles rolling her over, preventing her airway from being compromised in the water. Nanobots swiftly fixed the minor damage she had suffered.

Without this intervention, she would have died.

When Cara regained consciousness, she found herself lying on her back. Above her, snow-white clouds flecked the deep azure blue sky, and the usual four-winged creatures occasionally flew across her field of view.

There was a deep rumbling on her left, followed by the ground shaking as another mushroom cloud expanded, rising slowly upwards, fire flickering deep in its depths.

Her aching muscles protested as she raised herself onto her elbows. What had happened? Where was Arx? She recalled reaching for him in the water and then, nothing.

At her feet, small waves broke and foamed onto the sand, and there, lying next to her, lay Arx, the bright sunlight glinting from the silver surface.

'Arx?' she croaked, surprised at how weak her voice sounded.

There was no answer. The only sound was the waves breaking on the shore and the occasional animal shriek from deep in the forest behind her.

Her heart sank as a thought hit her; was he dead? Could it be, after all this time alone, she had finally found Arx, and he was gone? Broken and unrepairable like Mr Mapper? A single tear traced a path down her cheek.

She struggled to her feet, the pain in her muscles making it much more difficult than usual. She shuffled over to Arx and gazed down at the still silver orb.

She had touched the surface and had received a powerful electric shock. So maybe he wasn't completely dead. She pondered for a while, trying to decide what to do. She cast a glance at the dense forest, thinking of getting a stick or branch which she could use to move Arx away from the water. Then something occurred to her. Holding up her left hand, she gazed at the metal. Was it metal? She had never thought to ask. Surely metal couldn't be this flexible. Clenching her fist, she watched as the fingers curled inwards in exactly the same way as a normal, flesh hand. Metal conducted electricity. She knew that.

But if her prosthetic hand wasn't metal, then maybe she could pick up Arx with it.

It was a risk. She could find herself shocked again, maybe this time fatally. She hesitated, then quickly reached down before she could change her mind.

This time, there was no shock. Arx was cool to the touch, which she was sure wasn't normal.

Carefully, she gripped the basketball with her prosthetic hand and lifted. The above normal strength of her fingers allowed her to grip the dimpled surface. Holding it up, she examined it closely. There was nothing unusual. There were no dents or scratches and there were no discoloured patches. It looked normal. So why wasn't he functioning?

'Arx?' She projected a thought at the sphere, but there was still no answer.

It was entirely possible that he was dead, just like Mr Mapper. How cruel, she thought to herself. She had been so happy to see Arx, the thought of having him around to protect her and to talk to had filled her with joy, and now that joy was dashed. Squashed like a bug under foot.

She sighed and cast her gaze around to find her backpack. It was where she had dropped it, at the tree line, just a few paces away. Then, she froze. Something else was in the sand.

Further along the beach, in the wet sand, was a single footprint.

She snapped her head around, glancing quickly up and down the beach, but saw nothing unusual or different. There was no one else in sight, but if that was the case, then who did the footprint belong to? Could it be hers?

Holding Arx away from her body, she walked up to the footprint and examined it carefully. It was a real Robinson Crusoe moment, because the footprint was both human and not hers. There was someone else in this world and they were probably not friendly, because if they were, why didn't they show themselves? Cara looked up and down the beach once more and then at the forest. There was no sign of movement.

What should she do? As she stood there undecided, she became more and more convinced that something was very wrong about the situation. Any normal person would have showed themselves. Briefly, she considered calling out, but then changed her mind and went back to her backpack, where she gently set Arx inside. Then she hefted it up onto her back and secured the straps.

After one last look around, she turned and broke into a loping run along the beach, determined to put as much distance between herself and whomever left that mysterious footprint.

Cara ran along the shoreline for a solid two hours before coming to a stop. She assumed that she had put enough distance between herself and the stranger who, for some reason known only to themselves, had chosen not to show themselves. Never once did she wonder how she could maintain such a vigorous pace for so long. She figured that all her past travels and journeys had kept her in good physical shape. In reality, it was thanks to the device at the base of her spine that constantly adapted and supported her body's needs.

At the tree line, she made another small fire and cooked another lizard killed with her bracelet's weapon. While she ate, she contacted Mei and filled her in on the day's events so far.

'Why do you think they didn't show themselves?' she asked Mei.

'It is odd,' replied Mei. *'I'm not sure why someone would do that. And you're sure the footprint was human? And that it wasn't yours?'*

'Absolutely. It was larger than mine and it had five toes.'

'It was a barefoot? No shoes?'

'Yes.'

'Hmmm, very strange. Well, for what it's worth, I think you did the right thing.'

Cara nodded, stuffing another morsel of hot meat into her mouth.

'I'm glad you think so,' she replied. *'The issue is, what do I do now? Do I keep away from them or try to contact them?'*

'*Keep away,*' was Mei's immediate response. '*I don't want you taking any risks. Has there been any changes in the scenery? Is it still just the sea and the forest?*'

'*No change,*' Cara replied despondently. '*It all looks just the same. Even the weather hasn't changed, warm with a gentle breeze coming from the ocean. Those explosions are still happening, too.*'

Across the vast sea, she watched a single huge mushroom cloud rising slowly upwards.

'*There must be someone here setting off those explosions, right? They can't be natural, can they?*'

'*I think so,*' agreed Mei. '*There must be a civilisation somewhere, although setting off nuclear explosions seems reckless. I need you to be careful, my love.*'

Cara smiled, chewing at the meat slowly.

'*I will.*' She changed the subject. '*I wish Arx was working.*'

'*Me too,*' Mei replied. '*You were lucky that electric shock didn't kill you. Do you think he can be repaired?*'

'*Don't know.*'

Cara stood and kicked sand into the fire to put it out. She wiped her face and fingers on her t-shirt and picked up her pack.

'But I'm not leaving him. Trouble is, I think he can only be repaired back in the machine world where he came from. I don't think even Isabelle from the Starship could do it.'

She resumed her walk along the beach, feeling the warmth of the afternoon sun on her face and exposed skin. A gusty breeze from the ocean blew in, sending small particles of sand swirling around her legs.

'You could be right,' answered Mei. *'Besides, would you trust anyone else to repair him?'*

'No.'

As she walked, Cara and Mei continued their conversation for a while and then Cara suddenly stopped in her tracks.

Mei instantly felt Cara's shocked thoughts. *'What is it?'* asked Mei. *'What's wrong?'*

Cara strained her eyes to make out the distant horizon, where the bright sunlight and haze blurred her vision. In the distance, she could just see a needle-like tower piercing through the clouds, reaching high into the sky.

Chapter 3

'How far away is it?' asked Mei excitedly.

Cara shaded her eyes under the rim of her cap.

'Not sure. I can't tell how big it is and I'm not good at estimating distances, but it's got to be a long way. Maybe.' She hesitated. *'Oh, I dunno, fifty miles?'*

'So, only a couple of days away?'

'Maybe. It could be further than that.'

'But you agree that it's worth investigating?'

'Oh yes,' replied Cara. But then she had a thought. *'Do you think that the owner of that footprint came from the tower?'*

Mei went quiet for a while.

'It's entirely possible,' she replied. *'And if it is, you need to be very careful. We don't know their motives or who they are. All we know is that we have a footprint in the sand and a large tower miles away. The two things may, or may not, be, connected.'*

'I have a weird feeling that they aren't connected, and that footprint belongs to another outsider like me.'

'Mmmm, not sure about that, but let's go with it as a working hypothesis. So, what you should do is make your way to the tower, while keeping away from the footprint stranger.'

Cara nodded.

'And being very cautious as I approach the tower. We know nothing about the people who live here.'

'Absolutely!' replied Mei. *'You know how I feel about you and your adventures. You scare me to death with your near misses and close shaves. I wish you'd stayed in a safe world. But now that you're there in this one, you must continue. We don't have a choice. You can't stay there.'*

'I know,' Cara sighed. *'I wish I was with you instead of being stuck on this beach. It hurts.'*

Cara felt the familiar surge of Mei's love wash over her. It was a powerful force, like a wave crashing against her mind, overwhelming and all-consuming. The intensity of it brought tears to her eyes. She felt phantom arms embrace her, drawing her in close, ghost-like kisses caressing her cheek.

'Don't cry, my love. We'll be together one day.'

'Yes, but when? This is hard, Mei. It's so hard to keep going, to keep being positive. You're the only thing that keeps me going.'

'I know, my love. I wish I could be there with you, but you know I can't. But I'll help you in every way I can. Just keep going, something good will happen soon, it has to.'

Cara sniffed and wiped the tears away from her cheeks.

'I love you; you know that?'

She felt Mei's smile.

'Right back at you, my lovely girl.'

Cara resumed her walk along the beach.

Sometime later, she had no watch to check how long she'd been walking. The sun's edge touched the sea, and it grew darker. It didn't take long to light a fire - the lighter just barely striking. It was out of fuel. She deployed her bracelet once more, gutted an animal that was very like a small snake, and ate roasted cubes of surprisingly tender meat.

Once the sun had disappeared, alien stars appeared above, and she spent some time gazing up at them. Mei had long gone, leaving Cara alone once more. A sudden thought hit her, and she wished once more that Arx was alive and working. Then at least she would have someone to protect her and watch over her while she slept. She no longer felt safe. Although she had left the owner of that footprint far behind her, what if they caught up in the night? What if they attacked her while she was asleep?

There was one thing she could do, she realised. Something that she had only done once before. After laying out her bedroll, she slipped inside and then pressed the button on the underside of her bracelet. Immediately, three words appeared floating in her inner vision: OFFENCE, DEFENCE, OTHER.

She selected DEFENCE and watched the air shimmer around her as a defensive screen deployed in a two-metre circle around her. She knew the screen was impenetrable. Back in the Nandae world, it had protected her against energy and projectile weapons. She was certain that no one could touch her once it was deployed, but what she didn't know was how long it would remain working. Assuming that it used power from somewhere, surely it would run out at some point? Would it last all night? Would she be vulnerable after just a few hours?

There was no way to know. So resignedly, she closed her eyes and tried to sleep.

In the morning, Cara was both surprised and relieved to see that the curtain of force was still shimmering around her. She was impressed. Whatever it used for power, there was clearly plenty of it. A quick command dropped the screen as she sat up.

She was thinking of breakfast when she noticed the marks in the sand. Footprints. This time, not just one, but several.

A sense of apprehension filled her as she tracked the imprints in the sand. They came up the beach to where she had bedded down for the night. Then they circled around her as though someone had been pacing back and forth around and around her defensive barrier, before continuing into the distance further along the shore.

Someone had followed her and watched her sleeping. Her creep-o-meter shot into the red. Who would do that? And if she hadn't had her defensive screen up, would she be alive right now? She shuddered at the thought.

She gazed at the footprints heading along the beach. They were, of course, headed toward the tower. She would be following whoever had left them. As she thought of catching up with them and confronting them, her apprehension turned to anger; but common sense quickly replaced that anger. What would she do? Kill them? Of course not. But who were they and what were they doing? And why did they stay hidden?

These were all questions that she couldn't answer right now. Her stomach rumbled. She needed to eat, but then she remembered that her lighter had run out of fuel.

Chapter 4

The nausea took till mid-day to recede, although Cara was sure that most of it was in her mind and not real. Eating raw flesh was not her idea of a three-course meal, but needs must. She had to eat, and she had no fire to cook anything. But as she jogged along the shoreline, she resolved to rectify that. She was no Girl Scout, but she had seen enough documentaries on TV where people had made a fire. She would stop before it got dark and try her best to emulate them, although she was pretty sure that it wasn't going to be easy.

As she ran, the tower slowly drew closer. By now she could see that it was enormous, and that it was far more distant than she had first estimated. At this rate, she figured it would take another three days to reach its base. All the more reason to figure out how to start a fire. Three days of eating raw meat was not something she wanted to do.

She ran along the beach, her deep and steady breathing matching her powerful strides and taut muscles. The footprints ahead of her extended into the distance, marking her path as she continued to push forward. Surely it wouldn't be long before she caught up with whoever was ahead of her? And what would she do when she did? She wasn't sure, but she knew she was bored with this cat-and-mouse game. She was going to find out who it was and deal with the situation when it happened.

Deep in thought, she suddenly realised that the footprints had disappeared. She skidded to a halt in the sand and looked back along the beach behind her, where she noticed the footprints had made a sharp turn towards the forest. It appeared the person ahead of her had changed course and headed directly into the densely packed trees.

This seemed odd to her, because she knew how thick and unforgiving the trees and undergrowth were. A few days ago, when she had first arrived in this world, she had ventured into those dark depths, or more accurately, tried to. It proved to be totally impassable, filled with sharp vines that scratched and ripped at clothing and thick, rubbery tree roots that could trip you up or cause a sprained ankle. So how had the mysterious person coped with those conditions?

She walked back to where the footprints entered the forest and peered into the undergrowth, where she spied an unmistakable path lined with hacked bushes, vines, and branches. The mysterious stranger had cut their way through the densely packed vegetation. But why? Where did the path lead? And perhaps, more importantly, should she follow?

It didn't take long for Cara to decide. There was no way she was going to venture into that dark tunnel. There was no way of knowing where it led, and obviously, it was full of animals. It was far too dangerous.

A thought occurred to her. Had the stranger entered the forest to hide? Had they gone into the forest to wait for her to pass, so that they would be behind her again? Were they watching her right now?

Backing away, Cara looked along the beach towards the tower and then back at the forest. Was she being stupid? If she continued to the tower, would she end up being trapped between the people who lived there and the stranger behind her? But then, what choice did she have? The tower was the only sign of civilisation that she had seen since arriving in this world. She had to investigate it. It was the only thing she could do. She couldn't stay on this beach forever. A decent meal and help were what she needed. She hoped that the tower's occupants were friendly.

She sighed and resumed her jog along the shoreline, determined to put as much distance as possible between her and the stranger. It wouldn't be enough, she knew. She would have to stop well before sunset in order to light a fire and eat. The stranger would surely catch up with her once again as she slept. Just the thought of it made her feel sick and anxious.

It took over an hour to light a fire and cook an evening meal. Eventually, she perfected a method of using a long stick and rotating it rapidly between her palms with the pointed end against a flat piece of wood. It took a lot of effort and wasn't quick, but it got the job done.

As the sun lowered towards the ocean, Cara ate and discussed the day's events with Mei.

'So, you still haven't seen anyone?' asked Mei.

Cara shook her head.

'Nope, they're obviously hiding from me. But why?'

'I don't like it,' replied Mei. *'It's fucking weird.'*

'Yes, it most certainly is,' agreed Cara.

She popped another hot morsel of meat into her mouth and chewed, slowly savouring the flavour. It wasn't too bad. It tasted a bit like a cross between chicken and pork, and obviously much better than the raw meat she had been forced to eat that morning.

Suddenly, a voice from the beach behind her made her jump.

'Hello?'

She snapped her head around to face the greeting to see a man standing ten metres away. His appearance shocked her. Long, greasy and matted hair reaching his shoulders framed a face covered in painful looking red sores. A long, scraggly beard covered his chest and a ragged, dirty shirt hung loosely from his shoulders. Dried blood crusted over deep scratches covering his bare arms. His legs were in no better condition, covered in long cuts and caked in yet more dried blood.

Mei quickly picked up on Cara's alarm.

'Let me see!' she commanded, pushing into Cara's mind.

Complying, Cara allowed Mei's mental presence to slip into her mind with practiced ease, where it fitted snuggly like a glove.

'What the hell's wrong with him?' she asked.

'Probably radiation and exposure to the elements. Looks like he's been here for a while,' replied Mei. *'Some of those scratches look deep and new. Do you think he got them from entering the forest, perhaps?'*

'You mean the footprints that entered the forest, don't you?'

'Uh, huh. I think this is the person who's been following you. Be careful. Don't let him get near.'

Cara stood and backed away from the stranger.

'You think he's dangerous? He looks old!'

'He's not old, I'll admit he looks it. He's about the same age as you.'

'What? He can't be. He looks ancient! Why do you think that?'

'Do you understand English?' asked the stranger, taking a step towards Cara.

'Stop!' shouted Cara at the approaching figure.

'Don't let him get close!' Mei shouted in her mind.

'You already said that!'

'Well, make sure you listen!'

Cara couldn't help grinning to herself, which she hoped that the dishevelled stranger didn't take as an encouraging gesture.

'I have Kates bracelet. If he tries anything, I'll use it.'

Even as she said it, she wondered if she could do it. Could she kill a person? It wouldn't be like killing for food. This would be taking someone's life. She wasn't sure that she could. The thought of it made her feel sick. Of course, she had her defensive screen, which she could deploy anytime. Nothing could get through that. So she didn't feel too worried or unsafe. She knew she could handle anything, especially a strange man who looked as though he could barely stand.

Just in case, she quickly pressed the hidden stud underneath the bracelet. The menu dutifully appeared, the large uppercase words hanging in the air before her, ready to be activated. Immediately, she felt Mei's relief in her mind.

'Good girl!' said Mei.

'You understand English,' stated the stranger. He cast a glance at her fire and the meat on sticks. 'Could I have some?' he asked, his voice almost pleading.

'First, tell me why you've been following me?' Cara asked.

'I haven't been following you,' was the reply. 'Please, can I have some food? I haven't eaten in days.'

Cara nodded and watched warily as the stranger limped over to the fire, where he sank to his knees, grabbing the hot meat and stuffing it into his mouth.

'He's lying,' said Mei.

'Obviously,' replied Cara. *'But why? What would be the point?'*

'Unless he's got something to hide?'

'He's not lying about not having eaten. Look at him.'

They both watched as he greedily filled his mouth again and again, grease and bits of meat running into his long beard.

'What should I do?' asked Cara.

'Find out why he's here and why he's following you. Don't trust him, no matter what he says.'

'Don't worry, I'll be careful. I'm not about to take anything he says at face value.'

'If I was there, I'd be able to tell if he was lying,' complained Mei bitterly. *'If only your Assist wasn't broken.'*

'If you were here, then things would be very different.' Cara smiled. *'Just think, the two of us alone on a beach in the sunshine and a warm ocean. I would love that!'*

'*You betcha!*' Mei replied, unable to prevent her desire, love, and lust from flowing into Cara's mind and body. Cara couldn't help flushing with excitement and reciprocated desire, and for a moment the two women allowed their minds to join, their thoughts becoming one.

When they separated, and Cara was able to refocus her attention in the real world, she was disconcerted to find the stranger still kneeling by the fire, staring intently at her.

'Thank you for the meat,' he said, all the while staring unblinkingly, his eyes flicking back and forth from her face to her chest.

Cara gritted her teeth and did her best to ignore the stranger's gaze.

'Who are you and why are you following me?' she asked.

'I'm not following you.'

'I don't believe you. You're lying.'

The stranger didn't reply at first, and Cara noted his poor physical condition as he struggled to get to his feet. He seemed to be quite weak. His hands were trembling, and his legs could barely support him.

'I'm not lying,' he replied, his right hand reaching behind him.

Cara tipped her head to one side.

'He is,' Mei's thought cut in.

'Of course he is,' answered Cara. *'But why? This whole situation is crazy. I don't understand what's going on.'*

'Me neither. But I know that he's a snake. First, he follows you, and he denies it and then he shows up begging for food. I don't like him.'

'Snap,' replied Cara. *'What should I do?'*

'If he makes a move, kill him!'

'I'm not sure I can do that!' replied Cara. *'Besides, look at him. He can barely walk!'*

'True. But I don't want you to hesitate. You've got to do it. Think about it. Why has he been hiding and why is he lying? He wants something. If he comes at you, use your bracelet and kill him!'

Cara was a little shocked at Mei's outburst. She knew Mei worried about her safety and that Mei had killed before in many battles. But she wasn't Mei. Could she find it within herself to do what needed to be done?

'Do you have more food?' asked the stranger.

Cara shook her head.

'Who are you and why are you here?' she asked.

'I'm really hungry.'

Cara frowned. The stranger was evasive, as well as a liar. As the sun began to set on the horizon, the light faded. She weighed her options. Being alone with this man in the dark was not an option. She didn't trust him. His behaviour was decidedly odd.

'If you're not going to answer my questions, then you're not welcome. Walk away, make your camp further along the beach away from here.'

He stared at her, his eyes moving up and down her body.

'I don't like the way he looks at me,' Cara told Mei.

'Me neither,' she replied.

'How about I take everything you've got?' the stranger asked in a menacing tone, withdrawing a very long knife from behind his back.

Chapter 5

She didn't kill him.

Instead, she waited, watching him limp towards her, waving the knife in front of him. It was kind of pathetic; she thought to herself. He was in no condition for a fight, no matter what he thought. When he was close enough, she quickly stepped forward and delivered a swift kick to his groin.

He doubled over, clutching himself between the legs, and collapsed to the sand. She watched without sympathy as he gasped and moaned, writhing in pain.

'Good girl!' exclaimed Mei in delight.

'Well, I'm not going to be robbed by a prick like him!' answered Cara. *'Look at him. He's pathetic. He thinks he can follow me, eat my food and then take my stuff! Not a chance!'*

She turned away from him and walked back to the now dwindling fire. Picking up her pack and belongings and resumed her march towards the tower. Behind her, she heard a weak, gasping voice.

'Wait!'

'Stop following me,' she called out over her shoulder. 'Next time I won't hold back!'

Cara was amazed at herself. The once timid and uncertain girl was gone. Replaced with a capable, resourceful and self-reliant woman. Though her journey had only spanned a few weeks, the challenges she had faced, the encounters with strange beings, the magic-like technology, and the worlds she had visited had all shaped her into this determined, world-travelling person.

'I'm proud of you!' Mei's love flowed into her.

Cara smiled.

'I love you.'

'And I love you.'

She kept walking until the sun had fully set before stopping and bedding down for the night. Once she had erected her defensive screen, she slid into her bedroll and closed her eyes. It took a long time for her to fall asleep. The questions and the day's events kept playing over and over in her mind. Who was that stranger? And why was he following her? But perhaps more importantly, who lived in the tower?

The morning was like every other. The sky was its usual deep blue, tiny specks of the strange birds high above, while on her right waves gently crashed and surged onto the shore. To her left, Cara could hear the usual squeaks and shrieks coming from deep within the forest.

But this morning was also different. Curled up in a foetal position some ten metres away, the stranger slept, his long knife beside him on the sand.

Cara paused and took a moment to observe the pitiful figure, almost feeling a twinge of pity for him. Then she turned and made her way into the shallow water, where she washed herself as best as she could. It didn't take long to collect her few things and stuff them into her pack. She rolled up her bedroll, attaching to her backpack, slung it over her shoulder and resumed her trek towards the tower.

'What about breakfast?' the stranger called out as she walked past him.

'Get it yourself,' she answered.

'Where are you going?'

Cara stopped and turned.

'To the tower. Do you know anything about it?'

He pushed himself up on his elbows.

'Don't!' he exclaimed with surprising strength in his voice.

Cara raised her eyebrows.

'Why not? Do you know the people who live there?'

The stranger shook his head, his obvious fear surprising Cara.

'No one lives there.'

'Then why shouldn't I go there?'

He couldn't maintain eye contact. His eyes flicked back and forth.

'There's something there, something terrible.'

'Something? What do you mean?'

'I don't know what it is. I just know it's there.'

Cara laughed.

'More lies?' she asked. 'Do you think that I'm going to believe you?'

She turned and resumed her walk along the beach.

'I'm not lying,' he shouted after her.

Cara ignored him. She intended to reach the tower as soon as she could. It was the only sign of civilisation she had seen. She had to find out what it was. The stranger was lying yet again, trying to stop her from reaching the tower. She wasn't going to let that happen. She would find out what was there for herself.

'You'll regret not listening to me! Don't go there! There's something there, I tell you!'

Cara walked on, no longer listening. She had a goal: she would reach the tower as soon as she could. She would face whatever was there - people, or the so called 'terrible something', or even nothing if it was empty.

As the day ended, Cara could make out the details of the tower. The long stretch of sandy beach ahead of her curved around to form a headland that reached for several miles into the crystal blue waters, at the end of which the structure stood tall and imposing. There was no sign of windows or doors.

She estimated it was still a day's walk away, but the thought of reaching it tomorrow filled her with excitement. Tomorrow she would find out who occupied this world. She would make friends and get help. She could finally sleep in a bed and get a decent meal. Maybe they had portals like the Nandae and she could get off this world. At last, she felt as though she was making actual progress.

She made camp and a meal, eating her fill of a blackened snake-like animal that had six legs while watching the sun touch the ocean as it set. This is a beautiful world, she thought to herself, or it would be if she were not lost and on her own. The stranger didn't count. Whoever he was, he was a nobody. Someone who followed you wouldn't reveal anything about themselves and then try to steal from you wasn't worth the time thinking about.

It had been a long and eventful day. When the sun dipped below the horizon, she was already in her sleeping bag chatting with Mei. It took a long while for her to drift off to sleep, her mind still buzzing from the events of the day and the anticipation of tomorrow.

In the excitement, she forgot to erect her defensive screen.

Chapter 6

An intense pain in her head awakened Cara.

For a moment, she didn't know where she was. Opening her eyes, she realised it was early morning, the first rays of the sun filtering through the trees to her left. Screwing up her eyes and wincing at the pain, she brought her hand up to her forehead and was surprised to feel a sticky substance. Was it blood? What had happened? What had hit her with enough force to cause her head to bleed?

Then, through the pain, she remembered where she was, instantly recalling that she had forgotten to erect her defensive screen.

'Who's in charge now, bitch?'

Realisation and fear kicked in simultaneously as she understood what was happening and who was talking. The stranger had returned.

Pushing up on her elbows, she saw him looming over her, his wicked knife in his right hand.

'Get up!' he growled at her, brandishing the knife.

Even though fear coursed through her veins like ice water, Cara knew she could handle the situation. She had Kate's bracelet. Pretending to be in more pain than she actually was, she struggled to her feet while surreptitiously pressing the hidden stud underneath the blue gem of her bracelet. The familiar words appeared hanging in the air in front of her: OFFENCE DEFENCE OTHER. All she had to do was select OFFENCE and the stranger would die.

'Take off your clothes,' the stranger told her, backing away, the knife held out in front of him.

'What?' asked Cara, shocked at the request.

'You heard me,' he replied. 'You asked me earlier who I was and why I'm here. Well, let me tell you. This,' he waved the knife around. 'Is Chara. It's an exile world.'

'What's that?'

'It's a world where criminals are exiled,' he smiled evilly. 'Can you guess what my crime was?'

A terrible thought hit Cara. The word OFFENCE hung large in her vision, almost begging her to select it. She shook her head.

'I killed thirty-four women.'

Cara's worst thought was confirmed, yet she couldn't bring herself to select the weapon. The thought of killing a human being, even one as despicable as this one, made her feel sick to her stomach.

'Do you know why they exile criminals here?' he continued, a lopsided grin on his face.

Cara shook her head once more.

'Because there's no one here and there's no way out.'
'What about the tower?' Cara nodded towards the tall structure.

The stranger grimaced.

'There's something there, I'll give you that. But I was telling the truth yesterday. Whatever it is, you don't want to meet it.'

She shook her head slowly. Ignoring the rumbling and the shaking ground as on the horizon, a giant mushroom cloud rose into the sky.

'I know I'm not going to last much longer.' He gestured with his knife to the ocean. 'The radiation will finish me off soon. But before I go, I'm going to have one last bit of fun.' He grinned his evil grin once more. 'With you.'

Adrenalin surged in Cara's veins, and her heart beat faster. She let her gaze drift to the words hovering in her vision. She would have to do it; she would have to kill him. There was no choice.

'Take off your clothes,' he said once again.

Cara hesitated, watching as he turned his head sideways to spit blood onto the ground. He was disgusting. If anything, he looked worse than yesterday. One of the red sores on his face was leaking, a red rivulet running down his cheek into his beard.

'I said,' he stepped towards her, brandishing the knife once more. 'Take your clothes off!'

She drew in a deep breath, about to select OFFENCE, when she heard a loud bang.

A look of surprise and shock appeared on the stranger's face as red blossomed on his chest. He took one staggering step sideways and then toppled forward onto his face, to lie still. Blood slowly pulsed out of a large hole in his back, running down his sides to soak into the sand.

Cara stood open mouthed, not understanding what had happened. As the blood stopped flowing, things clicked into place in her head. The stranger had been shot! But by whom?

Casting a glance up and down the beach, it didn't take long to find out. Twenty metres away, in the opposite direction of the tower, a figure lay sprawled on the sand.

Selecting DEFENCE, Cara watched the shimmering pale blue shield appear around her. After establishing the screen, she strode slowly and cautiously towards the prone figure.

She came to a sudden halt, her eyes drawn to the wild blonde hair and the camouflage clothing. A weapon lay on the sand, beside their right hand, fingers stretched out towards it.

'Cheryl!' screamed Cara, breaking into a run, throwing herself down beside the figure.

Cheryl's eyes flickered open.

'Cara,' she croaked, a crooked smile on her face.

Cara knelt by Cheryl's side, gently cradling her head in her arms. Brushing away the trademark long blonde hair that had fallen across her face, she gasped at the sight of Cheryl's flushed skin and the angry sores and rashes covering her arms.

'Cheryl!' Cara repeated. 'Are you okay?'

She made no attempt to stop the tears from running down her cheeks.

'You saved me!' she told Cheryl between sobs.

Cheryl closed her eyes, her smile fading.

'Well, someone had to!' she replied weakly.

'Oh Cheryl, I've missed you. Where have you been?'

'Looking for you.'

Cara stroked Cheryl's head gently.

'Well, you found me! And just in time. I think creep thought he was going to rape me!'

Cheryl's lips curved upward.

'He doesn't. Sorry. Didn't. Know what you are capable of. Please tell me you were about to kill him.'

Cara nodded.

'I didn't want to, but I had no choice. I was about to, then you shot him.'

Cheryl's eyes opened, locking onto Cara's with an intense expression. She grasped her arm with surprising strength.

'Good girl. Be strong. You're going to have to make tough decisions on your journey. Promise me you'll be strong in case I don't make it.'

Cara felt shocked.

'What do you mean? Of course you're going to make it. I'll cook some food and you'll be right as rain.'

Cheryl smiled wanly.

'I have radiation poisoning, Cara. A meal won't fix it. I'm not sure that anything can.'

'No!' Cara cried in anguish. 'We've only just found each other! There can't be that much radiation. Look at me! I'm okay! You're just tired and weak. You'll be fine!'

Cheryl's eyes searched Cara's face and then moved down to view her arms and upper body.

'You do look good,' she acknowledged, her eyebrows drawing together and her forehead creasing. 'How have you managed that?'

Cara wiped away her tears with the back of her hand.

'Like I said, there isn't much radiation, and I've been cooking things and eating meat. I've been looking after myself.'

Cheryl's expression changed, her eyes widening.

'No, that's not it. It couldn't be, unless.' She paused and then spoke again, her voice becoming stronger and more urgent. 'Unless you had help!'

Cara almost laughed.

'What are you talking about? There's only you and me here.'

Cheryl gripped Cara's arm once more, her expression growing hopeful.

'Help me over to the trees and I'll explain.'

Chapter 7

After Cara helped Cheryl to the tree line, she lit a fire, then killed and gutted a six-legged reptile the size of a small dog. Soon, she joined Cheryl, eating roasted chunks of meat.

Cheryl barely touched her food, saying that she felt sick. She propped herself up against a sturdy tree trunk. She looked far from healthy. Cara was worried when she noticed one blister on Cheryl's left arm, oozing blood. The rest of her bare skin was also red and blistered. She was clearly ill. Not as bad as the now dead stranger, but it was similar. Was Cheryl right about the radiation? Had the stranger been here longer and was therefore in a worse condition? Would Cheryl suffer the same fate?

'What can I do to help?' she asked Cheryl, desperate to do something for her.

Cheryl blinked with heavy eyelids and smiled thinly.

'I think that your implanted device might be the answer.'

When Cara looked puzzled, she continued.

'The device that the Machines implanted.'

Cara was silent. She frowned, then her eyes went wide.

'You're telling me that there's something inside me?' she exclaimed, her face twisting into an expression of disgust and disbelief.

Cheryl nodded.

'Arx told me. I noticed something strange about your behaviour when we were on the Nandai moon, so I asked him. He told me you knew you had a device implanted at the base of your spine, but you didn't know its function and that you'd be upset if you knew, so he didn't tell you.'

'What?' Cara exclaimed. 'That's total bullshit! I knew nothing about it.' Unconsciously, she moved a hand to the small of her back. 'I knew I couldn't trust those machines!' she said bitterly.

Cheryl gave a small, tired smile.

'They did it for the right intentions. They were trying to protect you.' She paused. 'And by the looks of you, it's doing a good job. Look at you.' She gestured weakly at Cara. 'You look almost as good as new!'

Cara was not impressed.

'They shouldn't have done it without permission! It's an invasion of privacy! They even asked me on the Machine world if I wanted to be fitted with what they called 'enhancements', cos they said that I was 'fragile', and I said no.'

She sat down heavily next to Cheryl.

'But you're telling me they went ahead against my wishes, anyway!'

Cheryl laid a hand on Cara's arm.

'Don't blame them. What they did was wrong, but right now, it might just help me.'

Cara shot her a puzzled look.

'What do you mean?'

'Well, obviously, I know nothing about the device or how it works, but it's possible that it uses nanobots.'

Cara shot her a puzzled look.

'Nano what?'

'Tiny microscopic machines. If I'm right, your bloodstream would be full of them.'

'Oh, for fuck's sake! Now you're telling me it's not just one machine, it's hundreds!'

Cara was not happy with this new revelation.

'Billions,' corrected Cheryl.

Cara's mouth hung open; her words frozen on her tongue as she processed the gravity of the situation. She shuddered at the thought of countless machines coursing through her veins and organs, a foreign presence invading her very being. What were they doing? What could they do? Could they control her? It sent chills down her spine and made her skin crawl. As soon as Arx was repaired, she vowed to have a serious conversation with him about removing these 'things' from her body. The thought of them sent a wave of revulsion through her, and she couldn't wait to rid herself of them.

'Don't think of it right now,' Cheryl told her, as if knowing what Cara was thinking. 'Besides, I might be wrong, but I hope I'm not, cos it might be the only thing that can save me.'

'What are you talking about?' Cara was angry. 'How can these things help you? They're inside me!'

Cheryl nodded slowly; her eyes half closed.

'You're right, they're inside you. But if we could get them inside me, they might repair the cell damage. Clearly, something is keeping you healthy.'

'So what are you suggesting? A blood transfusion? Good luck with that! We don't have the equipment!' Even though she wanted to help, she didn't see how it would be possible. 'I want to help. You know I do, but I don't see how.'

Cheryl leaned her head back against the trunk of the tree.

'We can't manage a transfusion. We don't even know if we're the same blood type, so a transfusion would probably kill me.'

'Then how?' asked Cara. 'How do we get the nano things into you?'

'The only way I can think is wound to wound. We would have to injure ourselves and allow the blood to mix. That way, maybe some nanobots could transfer into my bloodstream.'

Cara almost laughed.

'You've got to be joking! That would never work. Would it?'

Cheryl turned her head and locked eyes with Cara.

'It's the only chance I have Cara. you're right, it might not work. But without medical treatment, I'm going to die.' She gripped Cara's arm tightly. 'Will you do this thing for me? Will you give me a chance to live?'

Cara searched Cheryl's face, seeing hope, desperation, and strength. She could see that she meant it.

'I'll do anything, you know that,' Cara replied with a quivering voice. Her eyes brimming with unshed tears. 'I've been lost and alone for days. I've finally found you. I'm not going to let you leave me again.'

She placed her hand on top of Cheryl's.

'You're my friend. You saved me from that creep. If I can save you, I will.'

Cheryl sighed and closed her eyes. A single tear ran down her cheek.

'So,' Cara asked brightly, wiping her face with the back of her hand. 'How do we do this?'

'I think the easiest thing would be if we lie next to each other. If you put your arm on top of mine and allow your blood to run onto mine...' her voice broke off.

'We would have to cut our arms,' Cara finished for her.

'It won't hurt me. I can turn off the pain receptors in my arm.'

'But it would hurt me, I can't do that, my Assist is broken,' replied Cara. 'How much blood are we talking? It's not going to be a small cut, is it?'

Cheryl grimaced.

'No, the more blood mixing we can manage, the better.'

Cara sat back and considered. This wasn't going to be easy. It sounded extreme, but if Cheryl thought it might work, then it was worth giving it a try. Then she had an idea.

'Mei!' she shouted.

Cheryl opened one eye and gazed across at Cara.

'Mei can block the pain for me,' Cara explained. 'She did it once before when I was badly burned in the Empty World.'

'She can do that?' asked Cheryl. 'I knew the bond between the two of you was special, but I've not heard of that before.'

'Mei,' Cara projected a thought.

Mei replied instantly.

'I'm here, my love. Are you at the tower?'

'Not yet, but a lot has happened, and I need your help.'

Cara quickly brought Mei up to date with the morning's events. Unsurprisingly, Mei was concerned that Cara had come so close to being killed yet again.

'For goodness' sake Cara!' she exclaimed. *'Why didn't you kill him straight away?'*

'I was going to. I was close to it, but I kept hesitating. I've never killed a person before. It's bad enough having to kill animals to eat!'

'Sod the animals! He was a monster! He was going to rape you!'

'I know,' replied Cara. 'In the end, Cheryl did it for me. She's much stronger than me.'

'I want you to tell me you would have done it yourself if Cheryl wasn't there. Tell me you would have killed him.'

'Don't worry, I definitely would, and I promise you I will if it ever happens again.'

'Good,' Mei replied, relief obvious in her tone.

'What do you think of Cheryl's idea?' Cara changed the subject.

'Well, I can see what she's trying to do. I don't know any more than her about your implant. She's right about you being healthy compared to her, so it makes sense that the device is actively doing something, and I suppose it might use nanobots, or their equivalent.'

Cara couldn't help shuddering again at the thought.

'Then I need your help, like you did on the Empty World. I don't think I'll be able to cut myself.'

Mei was silent.

'Mei?'

'*Are you sure you want to do this Cara?*' Mei asked. '*It's more dangerous than you think. It would be really easy to cut an artery. If that happened, then we would struggle to stop the bleeding. You could die.*'

'*I hadn't thought of that,*' admitted Cara. '*But if I don't do this, Cheryl says she'll die. I can't just sit here and watch that happen!*'

'*Do you believe her?*' asked Mei. '*That she will die?*'

Cara studied Cheryl closely. She had closed her eyes once more. Strands of her long, blonde hair were plastered to her face, which looked flushed and swollen. A string of blisters ran from her forehead, down her cheek and onto her neck to disappear under her camouflage shirt. Her arms fared no better. They were covered in painful-looking red blisters. Obviously, she wasn't her usual active self. She seemed exhausted and worn out, and that, coupled with her not eating, was not a good sign.

It was clear to Cara that she had to do something.

'*Yes,*' she replied firmly. '*I do. She doesn't look good. I'm no expert. She could be right. And she looks like she has what the creep had. I'd say that she's only going to get worse. Can radiation do that?*'

'*Yes,*' came Mei's reply. '*From what you've told me, it sounds like it. Given that you keep seeing those explosions, even though they're far away, they're probably giving off a lot of radiation. Enough exposure will kill, eventually.*'

'Then I have no choice. I have to save her.'

Mei reluctantly agreed.

Cara turned to Cheryl.

'We're going to give it a go. Mei's agreed to help me. I can't do it on my own,' she explained.

Cheryl's red-rimmed eyes gazed at Cara with obvious relief.

'Thank you, Cara,' she said sincerely. 'Please thank Mei for me. I know she's probably worried about you.'

Cara smiled and nodded.

'She's always worried about me. Let's get into position before I think too much about what we're going to do.'

She helped Cheryl into a prone position on her back next to the tree, retrieved her sharpest knife from her backpack and lay down beside her, placing her right arm on top of Cheryl's.

'Ready Mei.'

'Put up your defence screen first,' Mei instructed her. *'We don't want to attract any animals with the smell of the blood.'*

Cara complied and soon the air shimmered a pale blue around the two women.

'Done.'

'Okay, relax and let me in.'

Cara complied and felt the familiar presence of Mei push into her mind. For a brief second, their thoughts merged in a loving embrace, then they separated.

'I love you,' said Cara.

'I love you too,' replied Mei as their minds merged and intertwined. She dived deep into Cara's control centres, forging an unbreakable connection between them. In this moment, all walls and barriers melted away as they became a single entity, united in mind and soul. Every thought and emotion, every sensation and desire flowed freely between them as Mei took complete control of their shared existence. It was a merging willingly taken and freely given, built on a bond of love and trust that could never be broken.

Mei/Cara turned her head to Cheryl.

'Cheryl,' she said simply.

Slowly, Cheryl turned her head, locking eyes with Mei/Cara.

'I'm going to do what you suggested. It feels like it might work but know this. I won't put my Cara at risk. I love her more than anything and I'll do anything to protect her. If she's in any danger, I'll put a stop to this, even if it means your death.'

Cheryl didn't even blink.

'Hello Mei,' she smiled weakly. 'I wish we could have met in better circumstances. I understand what you're saying. I'd do the same in your position. I just hope it works.'

'Me too. Are you ready?'

Cheryl closed her eyes and whispered, 'Yes.'

Mei/Cara raised her left hand holding the knife, brought it across her chest, and lowered it to Cheryl's arm.

Chapter 8

Bright red blood pulsed rhythmically from the deep gash in Cara's arm, slowly trickling and dripping onto a matching wound on Cheryl's arm. The metallic smell of iron filled the air as the thick, sticky substance coated their skin and stained the ground beneath them. Each drop carrying with it the hope that Cheryl would be cured by the tiny, microscopic machines that filled Cara's blood. Their arms were intertwined, their wounds merging into one as they lay next to each other, waiting silently while their blood mixed.

Above them, the four-winged birds wheeled around, catching thermals, soaring away accompanied by their harsh screeching. Waves gently broke onto the shore, hissing and foaming. The forest joined in with its own cacophony of rustling, screeching, and roaring.

The two women lay like this for a full hour before Mei/Cara declared that Cara had lost enough blood. After binding both wounds using lengths of material cut from Cheryl's camouflage trousers, Mei withdrew from controlling Cara's body.

'I can't do anything about the pain now that I have to leave,' she explained. *'Sorry about that.'*

'That's okay, I understand,' Cara answered, unable to stop wincing as Mei relinquished her control. *'I'll manage. I'll check on Cheryl, then make something to eat.'*

'I want you to take it easy for the rest of the day,' Mei told her. *'You've lost a lot of blood. You might feel a bit dizzy. Drink lots of water and don't exert yourself.'*

Cara grimaced.

'Water might be a problem. I've run out!'

'For fuck's sake Cara!' answered an angry Mei. *'You should've told me! You need to replace your fluids! If I'd have known you had no water, I wouldn't have agreed to this!'*

This was the first time that Cara had experienced Mei's anger. In all the time that they had been together, they had never exchanged a single harsh word. Until today. She couldn't help feel hurt and guilty for not informing Mei about her water supply. This was uncharted territory, a new dynamic in their relationship, and she didn't know how to handle it.

'I'm sorry Mei,' she said. *'I'll find water, I promise.'*

Mei was silent for a while.

'Cara, I know you're doing your best, but you keep putting yourself in these dangerous situations. I'm not sure if I want to scream at you or hug you.'

Cara smiled to herself.

'I'd love a hug right now, you know that!'

'Cara, I'm being serious! You need to be more careful! I've said this before, and I'll keep saying it. You keep scaring me to death with your adventures and the dangerous people you meet.' She stopped and then continued. 'I don't know what I'd do without you. You mean everything to me.'

'You know, I feel the same about you, Mei,' replied Cara. 'I try not to get into trouble, but it has a habit of finding me.'

'I know, you're a real trouble magnet and that's what worries me.' By now, the tone of her voice had changed from anger to concern. 'One of these days you're going to get yourself in a mess you can't get out of, or worse!'

'Don't ask me to stop trying to be with you, Mei,' Cara said firmly. 'I'm not going to stop until we're together, you know that.'

Mei sighed a big, long sigh.

'Please try to do a better job looking after yourself, and please stop scaring me.' The worry plain in her voice.

'I'll do my best, I always do,' Cara said emphatically, projecting love, warmth, and reassurance.

'So, how are you going to find water?' asked Mei, changing the subject.

Cara gazed over at Cheryl, who hadn't moved and appeared to be asleep.

'Do you think Cheryl's okay?' asked Cara, avoiding Mei's question.

'Well, I don't think we've made things worse for her, if that's what you mean. We must hope that there are nanobots in your blood and that enough of them have transferred to her. If they have, then they should work to repair her damaged organs right now. I think you should let her sleep.'

'Hmm. I really hope so. Do you think it would be alright to leave her?'

'Why?'

Cara twisted her face into an expression of disgust.

'I ought to do something with the creep's body. If Cheryl and I are spending the rest of the day and night here, then I should move it, otherwise it might attract predators. Not that I've seen any so far.'

'Good point,' replied Mei. *'But I don't want you exerting yourself. If the tide is going out, could you roll him into the sea and let it take him away?'*

Cara gazed over at the shoreline.

'That's a brilliant idea. And it looks as though the tide is going out. Some luck for a change!'

'Okay, I'm going to leave you now. I've just been called. Remember what I said. You need to rest and drink lots of water.'

'You've been called? Is everything okay?' Cara couldn't prevent her worry from leaking into their conversation.

'It's fine. This happens all the time. It's probably to listen to another announcement from Kate.'

Cara shuddered. She had heard enough tales from Mei about how horrible Kate was.

'Be careful. Keep out of her way, blend in, and don't stand out.'

It was Mei's turn to reassure Cara.

'Don't worry, I'm an expert at not standing out. I'll speak soon.'

In a flash, Mei was gone, a whirlwind of emotions and thoughts trailing behind her. Cara was left feeling empty, as if a part of her had been taken away. She sighed heavily; her gaze settling on the dead stranger lying face down in the sand.

She would dispose of the body and then find water. After that, she would rest with Cheryl. Hopefully tomorrow would bring good news and Cheryl would feel strong enough to make the journey to the tower.

She lifted her gaze to the distant edifice. Who or what lived there? Would they help? Could they help? Maybe tomorrow would tell.

Chapter 9

Cara's luck held. It proved to be easy to roll the body into the shallow water. He was thin and emaciated, and therefore much lighter than she expected. She watched as the water swept over the thin frame as it was pulled out with the tide.

Good riddance, she thought to herself. She felt no sense of regret and instead felt relieved that he was dead. After all, he had shown his true colours as a despicable human being. And he was dying anyway. She still wasn't sure that she could have done the killing herself. Cheryl had saved her from that decision.

Cara turned to look back at the trees. Cheryl was lying exactly where she had left her, underneath the canopy of leaves rustling in the breeze. Her chest rising and falling rhythmically, showing that she was still deep in slumber. Cara fervently hoped that if there were nanobots in her blood, they were doing their job and making her better.

She turned her attention back to the sand where she had left the stranger's meager belongings. There wasn't much, but there was a something that attracted her attention. A canteen. She had already checked - it was full of water. Even though she didn't relish putting her lips to an item that the stranger had drunk from, it was just what she needed.

She made her way back to the trees, where Cheryl was still sleeping peacefully. She drank as much water as she could, feeling a sense of relief and exhaustion wash over her. Her arm throbbed with pain, and she felt slightly dizzy. Judging by the position of the sun, it must have been around noon. There was nothing to do but to wait. It only took a few seconds for her to put up her protective barrier once again. Then she curled up next to Cheryl and closed her eyes.

When Cara awoke, she was surprised to see Cheryl sitting cross-legged beside her, her eyes fixed on the endless expanse of ocean.

'Hey,' Cara whispered.

Cheryl shifted her gaze from the sea and smiled down at Cara.

'Hey yourself.'

'Are you feeling better?'

'A little,' replied Cheryl.

Cara pushed herself up from the ground and settled beside Cheryl. The two women gazed out at the distant horizon, watching as the sun slowly made its way downwards to meet the sea. Its fading light cast a long, golden beam across the water. It would be dark soon.

'Thank you for what you did today. It was a very brave and selfless thing to do.'

'It was nothing,' replied an embarrassed Cara. 'You would have done the same for me.'

Cheryl glanced sideways at Cara.

'Don't be so sure. I'm not as nice a person as you.'

Cara sat in silence, unsure of how to respond to Cheryl's statement. It lingered in her mind. What did she really know about Cheryl? She was always the epitome of composure and professionalism, but what lay beneath that stoic exterior? What secrets did she carry and how did she end up on that starship with Kate, Joe, and the rest of the crew two worlds away from here? Come to think of it, where had she been all this time? Had she been lost like her?

'Do you have anyone special, Cheryl?' she asked.

Cheryl didn't answer immediately. She continued to stare at the endless expanse of ocean.

'Once,' she finally replied. 'A long time ago.'

Curious, Cara asked 'What happened?'

'He was killed,' she replied in an emotionless voice.

'Oh, I'm sorry,' answered Cara. 'I didn't mean to pry.'

Cheryl sighed.

'It's fine. He's long gone.'

Cara, never a big conversationalist, wasn't sure what to say. She was about to change the subject when Cheryl continued.

'He never returned from a mission on Kaunis. It was assumed that the enemy killed him, but we never found a body.'

They sat in silence for a while, listening to the waves and watching a flock of the strange four-winged birds fly past.

'You loved him?' Cara ventured.

Cheryl nodded, her movement slow and deliberate.

'He was the love of my life. It took me a long time to accept that I'd never see him again.'

'I can't imagine how hard that would be. The thought of losing Mei… Well, it's unthinkable.'

Cheryl tore her gaze from the ocean, a bittersweet smile on her lips.

'It's hell. Whatever you do, keep hold of Mei. Don't let her go.'

Cara grimaced.

'I'm doing my best. That's why I'm trying to get to her.'

The two women returned their gazes to the sea, watching the sun move lower and lower.

'Cheryl, why did you come with me when Kate asked you? You must have known that you would never get back. You've left everything behind.'

'I'm not sure, really,' came the reply. 'I could've said no. Kate wouldn't have forced me. I guess the more I thought about it, the more I realised that there was nothing for me in the new world. And there was something about you and your adventures that drew me in.' She turned to Cara and smiled warmly. 'Despite the fact that you were an annoying little girl!'

Cara laughed.

'Yeah, well, you're not the first person to call me that!'

They both laughed, and Cara put her arm around Cheryl's shoulders.

'I know I've already said it, but it's so good to see you and I'm so happy that my blood has helped you.'

'Seems like you have nanobots,' replied a smiling Cheryl.

Cara frowned. 'Yeah, I'm not so happy about that!'

'You should be,' said Cheryl. 'It's thanks to them you're so healthy. The machines must have really liked you.'

'I don't know about that. They wanted me to stay in their world. I had to convince them to let me go. I'm really pissed at them for putting something inside me against my will. I told them I didn't want them to do it, but they did it anyway! When Arx is repaired, I'm going to have it out with him!'

'Don't be so hard on him, he was…' Cheryl paused. 'Wait! Where is he? Is he lost like us?' She looked wildly around in search of the familiar silver orb.

'I found him two days ago,' answered Cara. 'He's not working, so I put him in my pack.' she nodded to her backpack lying in the sand nearby. 'Something happened when we went through that gate on the Nandae world. It broke him and split us all apart. I don't understand how. I thought I was alone. Alone and lost.'

'Yeah, something happened, that's for sure,' replied Cheryl. 'I was lucky to find your footprints in the sand. I've been following you for days.'

'And you turned up just in time,' Cara pointed out.

'I did, didn't I?'

Cara changed the subject when her stomach growled.

'Are you hungry?'

Cheryl considered, then said. 'I think I could eat.'

'Good.' Cara jumped up. 'Because it won't be long before it's dark, and it takes me ages to light a fire.'

Chapter 10

As usual, the next morning was no different from any other morning. Briefly, Cara wondered if this world had any other weather other than sunny and pleasantly warm. She had been on this world seven days now, or was it eight? She had lost count.

On the horizon there was a flash, followed by a ground shaking rumble. A white and grey mushroom cloud expanded and rose slowly into the sky. Once again, she marveled at the fact that the explosions had no effect on the local weather and conditions. How was that possible? It was just one more puzzle, probably never to be solved.

The two women ate breakfast, which Cara cooked in the usual manner.

'You seem better than yesterday,' Cara pointed out.

Cheryl nodded, chewing on a morsel of meat. 'I do feel a lot better.'

'Your rash looks less angry, too.'

Cheryl looked down at her arms.

'They seem a bit improved. They're less painful.'

Cara chewed thoughtfully on a piece of meat.

'When will we have to do the blood transfer again?'

'Well,' Cheryl licked her lips clean of grease and wiped her hands on her trousers. 'I think, and this is just a theory, I think the nanobots are reproducing themselves. So, if that's the case, we won't have to do it again.'

Cara couldn't stop the ear-to-ear grin appearing on her face. 'Thank God for that! Although,' she paused and furrowed her brow. 'The thought of millions of machines inside me reproducing makes me feel sick!'

'Billions,' replied Cheryl, laughing.

Cara huffed and changed the subject.

'You up for a walk,' she inclined her head towards the distant tower.

'You bet. We need to find someone to help us, if we can.'

'Given your condition, I reckon that it's a couple of days away.'

Cheryl shaded her eyes and looked along the beach towards the peninsular at the end of which, the tower stood tall and more than a little ominous.

'The dead creep told me that there's a 'thing' living in it,' said Cara.

Cheryl raised her eyebrows, turning her attention back to Cara.

'Thing?' she asked.

'Yeah, he went on about something living in the tower and that I shouldn't go there. I reckon he was trying to put me off. I think he was lying.'

Cheryl fell silent for a while, gazing at the distant tower.

'Hmm, I wonder.'

'What do you mean?' asked Cara.

'A couple of days ago I felt a presence coming from that direction,' she nodded to the tower.

'A presence?' Cara didn't understand what Cheryl was talking about. 'What's that?'

'It's a sort of byproduct of wearing an Assist. Sometimes you can 'feel' some people, especially those that have powerful minds. Didn't you always know when Kate was nearby?

Cara nodded thoughtfully. 'Yes, I hadn't really thought about it before.'

'Kate was the most powerful of all of us,' continued Cheryl. 'Even more than Joe.' She paused for a second, then carried on. 'Well, anyway, I sensed a powerful mind. I don't think it knew I was there or was looking for me.'

'Why would it be looking for you?' asked a fearful Cara. 'You're not suggesting that you were being hunted, are you?'

'No, no. I just got the impression that it was looking for something and it didn't care about me.'

'I don't understand. What are you saying?

'I'm saying that maybe the dead creep wasn't lying. Maybe there is something living in that tower.'

Cara gazed at the distant tower thoughtfully.

'I guess it doesn't really matter, does it? We must find out. We can't sit around doing nothing. We need to find people, if they exist, and there's only one way to do that.'

'Get to the tower,' Cheryl finished Cara's statement.

'Yup, and there's no time like the present. Shall we?' Cara stood, brushing sand from her legs.

Cheryl slowly climbed to her feet, joining Cara, staring at the tower.

'Sorry I'm not at my best, but I'll walk as far as I can.'

Cara smiled at her friend.

'Don't worry, we'll take it easy.'

Cheryl smiled back.

'Do we have time to clean up? I feel pretty dirty and smelly.

Cara took in Cheryl's greasy hair and sweat-soaked clothes.

'I think we have time for an essential wash.' She turned to the ocean and stepped towards the breaking waves. 'You coming?' she called over her shoulder.

The two women washed themselves and their clothes in the warm water. Cara couldn't help but notice the red skin and blisters that trailed down Cheryl's left side, from her cheek to her arm and all the way down her leg. It was clear Cheryl had been exposed to a large amount of radiation on this side of her body. Now that she saw the extent of her injuries, she understood why she had been so ill. The extent of the skin damage indicated that Cheryl had probably received a fatal dose. She had been right. In this world, with no cities and therefore no hospitals or doctors, her only hope was the nanobots.

Cara fervently hoped that the tiny machines were doing their job, and grudgingly had to admit to herself, she was glad that they were in her own body. She hadn't agreed to have them placed inside her, but right now, they were keeping her fit and healthy, and hopefully, they would continue to cure Cheryl, too.

They walked along the beach, Cara carrying both her own and Cheryl's backpack. They took frequent breaks and carried on until Cheryl was exhausted and could go no further. It was nowhere near the distance that Cara was used to completing each day, but it brought them closer to their objective. She estimated they were still two days away at this pace. Hopefully, that would give Cheryl time to recover and gain some strength. They might need it when they arrived.

That evening, Cheryl asked Cara to disassemble and clean her weapon. At first, Cara was dead set against it. She hated guns and didn't want to touch it. But Cheryl insisted.

'We don't know what we might find at the tower. We need to be prepared. I'm too tired to do it myself. It's important to keep weapons clean to prevent misfiring. It's been in the sand and been fired. It needs to be cleaned.'

According to Cheryl, her weapon was a Heckler and Koch MP5. While it wasn't the latest model of SMG available, it was her preferred choice. Cara couldn't help but feel disgusted at the idea of preferring any type of weapon. In her eyes, all weapons were inherently evil and should never be used. However, she couldn't deny that she was grateful when Cheryl had used it to shoot the stranger yesterday.

So reluctantly, she complied with Cheryl's request, carefully and cautiously following her detailed instructions until the task was done. Breathing a sigh of relief, she rubbed her hands back and forth on her shorts as if to wipe away the fact that she had handled a device capable of killing.

She distracted herself by cooking another lizard and was pleased to see that Cheryl ate more than she had before. It was a good sign; she thought to herself. Cheryl was getting better. Afterwards, they both slipped into their sleeping bags and slept, protected behind Cara's defensive screen.

Two days later, they were at the foot of the tower.

Chapter 11

The vast tower stretched high into the sky before them, an impenetrable block of solid and smooth blackness. There were no entrances or windows, not even a scratch marred its perfect surface.

The base was oddly shaped, with multiple sides of varying lengths. They had spent the last two hours circling it twice, desperately trying to find a way in, but had found nothing.

There was no way in.

'Shit!' Cara shouted. 'What a waste of time!'

She kicked at the obsidian wall in front of her, the sole of her boot finally coming off, flying high into the air.

'Fuck!' she screamed.

She sat down suddenly, her back to the tower, her head in her hands.

Cheryl, ignoring Cara's outburst, stood a little distance away, staring up at the top of the tower.

Cara had removed her boot and was examining the underneath, an expression of disgust on her face, when she noticed Cheryl.

'What's up?' she called. 'Can you see a way to get inside?'

Cheryl, standing still as a statue, didn't answer.

Cara frowned and then threw her now useless boot at Cheryl. It landed at her feet.

'Hey Cheryl!' she shouted.

Cheryl turned to face Cara.

'Can't you feel it?' she asked, her face pale.

'Feel what?'

'It's up there,' she pointed a shaking finger skywards.

'What is?' asked Cara, struggling to her feet. She hobbled over to Cheryl, hampered by one bare foot and one booted foot. When she arrived, she turned her gaze upwards to see what Cheryl was looking at, but all she saw was the featureless blackness climbing skywards, it's very top disappearing in the clouds.

'I can't see anything,' she said.

Cheryl shook her head.

'There's a powerful mind up there. I've felt nothing like it.'

'Well good,' replied Cara. 'Let's get their attention. Let them know we need help.'

'No!' hissed Cheryl. 'We don't know what it is. I can't believe that you can't feel it! It's enormous!'

Cara was surprised to observe that Cheryl was actually shaking, but she dismissed her misgivings. She was intent on contacting whatever it was. She was single-minded.

'I don't care how big the thing is. Let's get it to come out or open a door!' She limped back to the tower, grabbed a rock from the ground, raised her hand, and slammed the rock against the tower.

'No!' screamed Cheryl.

Cara ignored her and slammed the rock against the black wall once more. She raised her face upwards and shouted.

'You there in the tower! Come out, we want to talk with you!'

Cheryl slammed into Cara, knocking them both to the ground.

'Stop!' she shouted, but it was too late.

A massive mental force crashed into the two women. Cara screamed in pain, clasping her hands to her head.

'INTRUDERS.'

The mental voice smashed into her mind. Questing needles of thought probed deep into her very being, heedless of the damage they caused. They sucked at her memories, pushing her aside, leaving her no room to think, to marshal her thoughts, to resist. The massive, overwhelming presence filled her mind, ignoring her pain, absorbing everything in less than a second. She gritted her teeth against the agony as she felt its diamond hard probes exploring every recess, every niche, and every part of her. She even felt it travel down her spine, flooding every nerve with pain.

In the next second, she lost consciousness.

Cara awoke to the worst headache she had ever had in her life. A moan escaped her lips as she screwed her eyes tight shut and rolled over into a foetal position, desperately trying to escape the pain. It didn't help. If anything, the pain got worse.

She couldn't prevent another moan as she clutched at her head, pulling at her hair, rolling onto her back.

'Do you give permission for the removal of pain?'

Cara couldn't even think straight, let alone give permission. She struggled to breathe, gasping in short, shallow breaths as she rocked back and forth in agony.

'Lack of response and your obvious discomfort will be accepted as permission.'

She opened her mouth to scream, the pain now too much to bear, when suddenly it disappeared. The scream died on her lips and slowly, her breathing returned to normal. Removing her hands from her head, Cara slowly opened her eyes and was startled to find herself in a room that was very familiar. The orange walls and the glowing ceiling immediately conjured up a memory of the room in the Machine world.

At first, she was speechless, the memory of the pain in her head lingering along with the confusion of where she was. Then she spied the silver ball hovering beside her and couldn't help shouting out.

'Arx!'

She was surprised at how stiff her muscles were. And, exactly as she had been when she had first awakened in the Machine world; she was naked. Pushing herself up from the raised platform, she reached out to pull Arx to her, wrapping her arms tightly around him.

'Oh Arx, you're alive!'

Overwhelmed with emotion, Cara couldn't stop the tears of joy streaming down her cheeks. She laughed and cried, hugging the silver ball to her chest, murmuring his name repeatedly.

'Repetition of my designation is normal?'

Arx's voice was barely audible, wrapped in the embrace of Cara's arms.

'Yes! yes, it is! Arx, I'm so pleased to see you!' Tears of joy streaked down her cheeks.

'I must warn you that your efforts to crush me will fail.' Arx replied in his usual emotionless and mechanical monotone.

'I'm not trying to crush you! I'm hugging you, you idiot!' replied a laughing Cara.

'Hugging is significant?'

'Yes! You bet it is. I'm so happy that you're repaired!'

'Pleased is a human emotion?'

'Oh, for fuck's sake, stop asking questions and just accept that I missed you and I'm glad that you're back!'

Arx fell silent. Then suddenly, Cara released Arx, an expression on her face that was a cross between shock and puzzlement.

'Wait a minute!' she exclaimed. 'You're repaired! Who repaired you?'

Arx floated away to hover nearby.

'A repair was not required.'

Cara frowned; her lips pursed together.

'You must have been. You weren't working.'

'I was in stasis mode, implemented to conserve energy.'

'I won't pretend to understand what you just said, but are you okay now?'

'Affirmative. All my systems are running at one hundred percent efficiency.'

Cara breathed a sigh of relief and frowned once more after casting a quick glance at her surroundings.

'Where am I? Are we back in your world? This looks exactly where I woke in your world. And where is Cheryl?' Her voice suddenly got louder and more frantic. 'Where's Cheryl?'

'Please remain calm,' instructed Arx. 'Cheryl is safe. She is in the second facility.'

'What? Where?' Cara asked, alarmed.

'The second facility is on the fourth planet in this system.'

Chapter 12

'Please tell me that's not true! She should be here!' shouted Cara. 'She's not well. She needs medical treatment!'

Arx moved to one side and then back again.

'Cheryl is being repaired and will soon function at peak efficiency,' he replied.

Cara's mouth kept opening and closing like a gasping goldfish. Then, all at once, the words jumbled out of her in a rush as the questions came one after another.

'How is that possible? How did she get to another planet? How do you know these things? And how come you're repaired? Just what is going on here?

Yet more questions from an increasingly frantic Cara interrupted Arx as he tried to answer.

'Where am I?' she looked around; her eyes wide. 'How come this place looks like where I was in your world? Why did someone take Cheryl away?'

By now Cara was almost hysterical, her voice high pitched and her breathing fast.

'And,' she shouted up at the ceiling. 'Where are my clothes?'

She fell silent, panting, bringing her artificial hand up to her head, while gazing incredulously at the foam-covered platform she was sitting on. It was identical to the platform in the Machine world.

'Please remain calm,' instructed Arx. 'I will explain everything. Do you wish me to answer your questions in the order you asked them?'

'Remain calm?' she screeched. 'You must be joking!'

'I have no experience of joking.

Arx's typical response calmed her down somewhat.

'What happened to me and Cheryl? What was that thing that invaded my mind?'

'You are in no danger. My perceptors indicate you are agitated.'

Cara looked up at the silver ball, eyes narrowing, lips thinning in anger.

'Just answer my questions,' she growled.

'Very well. Cheryl is in no danger; her biological functions are being repaired. She is currently in a facility identical to this one on the fourth planet in this system. The Entity transported her.'
Before Arx could continue, Cara interrupted him.

'Entity? What's that?'

'The Entity resides in this complex. It is the only intelligence in this world.'

Cara gazed around the room warily.

'Where is it? Is it dangerous? Are we in the tower?'

'It is not dangerous, not in the sense you mean. It is very curious about you and how you came to be here. It has informed me it has encountered humans before, and it wants to learn more. Yes, we are in a tower construction.'

'Curious about me?'

'Yes. It cannot communicate with you directly. When it tried to do so, it overloaded your cognitive functions. It was this overload that caused your pain. It revived me from stasis and implanted systems within my internal framework to enable communication between us.'

Cara gasped.

'You mean it operated on you?'

'I have a new mechanism that enhances communication.'

'That's horrible.' Cara's mouth twisted into an expression of disgust. 'It,' she paused. 'It opened you up and put something inside you.' Suddenly she laughed. 'Oh, the irony. You did the same thing to me! We both have something inside us that was put there without permission!'

'The mechanism enhances my abilities. Your mechanism keeps you functioning at peak efficiency.'

Cara glared at Arx.

'We'll talk about that later. Now is not the time, but you should know that I'm not happy that you put something inside me!'

Arx moved sideways, then back again.

'What is this entity and what does it want with us? Why is it so interested in me?'

'I am not aware of its intentions.'

'You can talk with it?'

'Correct.'

'Then ask it!' Cara instructed in an exasperated tone. 'Why haven't you already asked?'

Arx moved from side to side again.

'The Entity states that it is interested in your species and that you appearing on this planet has provided an ideal opportunity to study you first hand.'

Cara felt a trickle of fear run down her spine.

'Oh, shit!' she whispered to herself.

'May I answer your remaining questions?' Arx asked in an emotionless monotone.

Cara nodded slowly, trying to digest the implications of Arx's last statement. Did it mean that she would be trapped in this room for the rest of her life? To be studied like a lab rat?

'The Entity created this room for you in order to provide a familiar environment.'

'How thoughtful,' she replied sarcastically.

Arx continued, ignoring her tone.

'The Entity has informed me that the equipment necessary for Cheryl's repair is on the fourth planet in this system. So she was immediately transported. Once the Entity confirms Cheryl's biological functions are fully repaired, the Entity will transport her back here.

'Oh. She'll be okay?'

'The Entity assures me it has experience repairing humans.'

Cara wasn't sure how to respond to that. It could be a good thing or a bad thing, depending on how you looked at it.

'Your protective layers were removed to facilitate the Entities study of your biological components. It appears the Entity is curious about the connections between non-organic and organic systems.'

Cara's anger flared at this revelation. No matter where she went, there was always someone or something poking around and examining her innermost self, whether it be her body or her mind, and always without her consent. It left her feeling violated and disgusted.

'Well, maybe it wouldn't be so interested if you hadn't put whatever it is inside me in the first place!' She was tired of being used and treated like an object.

Arx ignored her anger.

'Your protective layers are available if you still require them.'

Cara's mouth fell open. She was speechless for a full thirty seconds.

'Of course I want my clothes, you idiot! Why didn't you give them to me at the start?'

Arx moved sideways and then back again.

'I have difficulty comprehending your requirement to cover your natural form. But I have observed that Cheryl has the same preference, therefore I conclude it is a human characteristic.'

'No shit Sherlock!'

'I have no experience of Sherlock.'

Cara rolled her eyes.

'Just get my clothes. Now!'

A sudden gust of wind and a snap of sound saw a bundle of clothes appear on the platform next to her. She eagerly sifted through the garments and slipped on her underwear, T-shirt and shorts. As she did, a sense of comfort and familiarity washed over her, filling her with relief and a renewed sense of self.

Sighing quietly, Cara surveyed the room.

'I'm sorry that I've been so angry with you Arx, I really am pleased to see you.'

'I have no experience of please.'

Cara grimaced.

'I know. You've told me that before. What I mean is that I've missed you and it's good to see you again.'

'Missed is a human emotion?'

'Well, sort of, I suppose. I don't know how to describe it. I guess it means that I like being with you and didn't like it when you weren't there.'

Uncharacteristically, Arx was silent for a while.

'I do not understand human emotions. I can relate that I find our interactions stimulate new processes within my quantum substrate.'

Cara laughed.

'Maybe that's the same thing.' She gazed around the room once more.

'So, what happens now? Am I a prisoner?'

'The Entity informs me it wishes to observe you in your natural environment.'

Cara looked confused, her eyebrows drawing together.

'What's my natural environment? Not back on that beach that goes on forever, surely?'

'No, the Entity has advised that the environment on this planet is not conducive to humans. It is conducting experiments on the surface which involves radiation that is lethal to your biology.'

'I had noticed,' Cara replied wryly. 'It almost killed Cheryl. Speaking of which, when am I going to see her again?'

'The Entity will bring Cheryl here if you wish. She is now fully repaired.'

Cara clapped her hands with glee.

'Yes, yes! Bring her back!'

'Move away from the sleeping platform. Cheryl will be transported directly.'

Cara complied, waiting eagerly for her friend to appear.

She expected the usual snap of air, followed by Cheryl appearing on the platform. Instead, there was a bright flash causing her to squeeze her eyes tight shut. When she opened them, she gasped in shock.

Cheryl had not appeared. Instead, a woman with long auburn hair and glasses sat staring back at her.

She gave a small, sad smile and spoke.

'Hello Cara.'

Chapter 13

Cara studied the strange woman sitting on the platform in the centre of the room. She was wearing a simple white top, a short purple jacket and a pair of blue jeans. Her long auburn hair was unkempt and looked like it hadn't been brushed for a long time. Behind her glasses, emotionless hazel eyes stared back at her. On her right hand were the familiar golden rings of an Assist.

Where was Cheryl? And who was this woman? Had Arx lied? He had said that Cheryl would be transported back, not a stranger.

'Arx, who is this?' she directed her question at Arx, her gaze not leaving the stranger.

'I have no knowledge of this human,' Arx replied.

The stranger spoke up.

'I'm Molly. It's nice to meet you.'

'Where's Cheryl?' asked Cara warily. 'Why are you here?'

'She's fine. I wanted to see you. I don't get many chances to meet people in the flesh.'

Cara frowned, puzzled.

'I asked Ed, and he agreed. I think he's finally realised that isolation is not good for me,' Molly continued.

'I don't understand what you're saying. Where have you come from? What do you mean you don't get to see people?' asked Cara.

A brief flicker of a smile appeared on Molly's lips, which was quickly replaced by a sad expression.

'I'm sorry, I haven't explained myself. What has your mechanical companion told you so far?'

Cara cast a quick glance at Arx, who was hovering nearby.

'He hasn't said much. Something about Cheryl being repaired and an entity who lives in this tower.'

Molly nodded.

'I thought so,' she replied, reaching into a jacket pocket. 'Let me explain.' She withdrew a packet and a lighter, extracting a cigarette. She lit up and drew in a deep breath. 'Oh, sorry, would you like one?'

Cara nodded enthusiastically and reached to accept the proffered cigarette from Molly. She leaned forward, allowing Molly to light it for her. As she took a drag, she let out a satisfied sigh, enjoying the warmth of the smoke as it filled her lungs.

'Thanks.' She took another drag and blew out the smoke. 'I ran out days ago. I've been desperate ever since!'

Molly smiled another of her sad smiles.

'I can imagine,' she replied. 'So, to business.' She crossed her legs and pushed her glasses up her nose. 'Ed is who I call what your companion refers to as the Entity.' She glanced up at Cara. 'Well, I had to call him something. It was the first thing that came into my head.'

Cara stood next to the platform, listening intently.

'The first thing you should know is that you aren't in any danger. On the contrary, Ed's species consider themselves guardians. They do their best to preserve life. But they are very curious about us.'

'Arx told me that the Entity, Ed, was interested in me,' Cara interrupted.

Molly gave a little grunt while putting the cigarette to her lips.

'Interesting name, Arx. From a song?'

'Yeah, but one I've forgotten.'

Molly nodded. 'I've been here with Ed for almost two years. At least,' she paused. 'That's what I think. It's difficult to tell, with the lack of seasons and the different length of days.'

'Two years!' exclaimed Cara. 'How come? Were you kidnapped?'

'Nothing so dramatic,' Molly gave a small, bitter laugh. 'No. I volunteered to come here.'

'Volunteered! Were you mad? Who'd volunteer to come here?'

'Well, I didn't have much choice, it was me or,' Molly broke off, staring down at the remnants of her cigarette in her hand. She drew in a quavering breath and let it out. 'Or the love of my life,' she whispered.

A wave of empathy flowed through Cara as she quickly sat next to Molly, putting her arm across her shoulders.

'I'm sorry,' she said simply.

'It's okay, I did the right thing.' Molly flicked a glance across at Cara. 'Sally would never have survived this.'

Cara slowly blinked, feeling a surge of emotions wash over her. She felt empathy and sadness for Molly's selfless sacrifice for her partner, but she also experienced something she hadn't felt in a long time: a sense of kinship, a connection. It was clear that Molly was in love, just like herself. Without thinking, Cara pulled Molly into a hug, unable to resist the overwhelming connection between them.

For a while, the two women held each other close, words unnecessary.

'Connecting your bodies is a method of communication?' asked Arx.

Cara, being much more used to Arx's strange questions, laughed while Molly flushed bright red. The two women separated from each other.

'We aren't connecting our bodies,' explained Cara. 'We're hugging, just like I hugged you earlier. I suppose you could say it is a form of communication.'

Arx moved sideways and then back again.

'What information passes between you when you connect your bodies in this manner?' he asked.

Molly giggled.

'I'm not really sure,' laughed Cara. 'Let's just say that it feels good and leave it at that.'

'I have no experience of feel,' replied Arx.

'Let's get back to the point, shall we?' asked Cara.

Molly reached into her jacket pocket once more.

'Another?' she asked.

'Definitely,' answered Cara.

Once they had both lit up, Molly smiled at Cara.

'Thanks, I needed that. The hug I mean.' She blew smoke out towards the orange ceiling and then continued. 'Ed belongs to an alien species we call the Non'anan. They are ancient and very powerful. They've helped us.'

'You're talking about Earth?' Cara asked.

'Uh, huh. We found ourselves under attack twice. And it turns out the enemy was the same each time.' She took a drag from her cigarette.

'Bad Kate and bad Joe,' stated Cara.

Molly looked up, surprised.

'You know about them?'

'Yes. You see, I'm on a journey to be with the woman I love, Mei Xing. She lives in the same world as bad Kate and bad Joe.'

Molly's eyes were round, her eyebrows raised.

'Well now, no wonder Ed is interested in you. You've been hopping between worlds.' It wasn't a question, more a statement of fact.

Cara flicked ash onto the floor.

'Five so far. I'm determined to be with Mei, no matter what it takes'.

If it were possible, Molly's eyebrows rose even higher.

'That explains it. I knew there was something different about you. Parallel worlds are new to us. We don't know a lot about them. I headed up a project to build a detector. We wanted to detect if someone from another world entered our own. The project wasn't completed before I left to come here, but I discovered that world hopping changes the brain.' She brought up her cigarette to her lips. 'Did you know that your brain was different?' she asked.

Cara was mildly surprised that she wasn't at all concerned about this revelation.

'Well, I've got everything else. Why not an abnormal brain?' she answered sarcastically.

Molly took a long drag from her cigarette. 'I said different, not abnormal.' She shifted her cigarette to her left hand before raising her right towards Cara, the light glinting from the rings of her Assist. 'May I?' she asked, pausing for permission before touching Cara's forehead.

Cara felt a gentle pressure behind her eyes and at the back of her neck. Then nothing.

'Hmmm,' remarked Molly.

'What does that mean?' asked Cara. 'Is it bad?'

Molly chuckled.

'No, not at all. I wish I had you in my lab back on Earth. Your brain is extraordinary. I've seen nothing like it. I'd love to look deeper.' She sighed. 'But that's not going to happen. I'm stuck here for another year yet.'

'Well, I'm not sure that I want to have my brain examined, even by you.' Cara took a last pull from her cigarette before flicking it away. 'It doesn't matter, anyway. Why do you have to stay here for another year? Why not go back home?'

'I can't go back home Cara. We made an agreement. I volunteered to be with the Non'anan for three of their years.' She pulled her cigarette packet from her jacket pocket once more. 'I don't normally chain smoke,' she apologised. 'But this isn't an ordinary day for me.' She passed the packet to Cara. 'Seriously, your brain is unique, and I'd like to know why.' She paused to light up. 'I guess you wouldn't know that I was one inventor of the Assist.' She took a long pull from her newly lit cigarette. 'You've met Joe? Well, I was one of Joe's first recruits. He came to me for help to develop it into a wearable device.'

She reached over to take Cara's right hand and examined the rings on her fingers.

'Interesting,' she murmured. 'The thumb and little finger rings are missing. Its functions must be seriously degraded.'

'They are,' answered Cara. 'I can talk to Mei, but that's all.'

'And this?' asked Molly, running a forefinger over the small ring on Cara's little finger. 'I can feel that it's somehow connected to your Assist?'

'Kate gave it to me,' Cara explained. 'It allowed me to talk to Mei from the Starship.'

Molly shot a glance at Cara, her eyebrows raised once more, then looked back down at Cara's wrist.

'This is special too,' she squinted down at Cara's bracelet.

'That was another gift from Kate. I didn't want to take it, but she insisted. Good job too. it's saved my life more than once. I don't know how it works. I use it for protection, and it can also kill.'

Molly released Cara's hand and put her cigarette to her lips.

'You also have an artificial hand?'

Cara raised her left hand up to the light, flexing her fingers and rotating her wrist.

'Some insect stung me. The machines told me that my hand was gone, so they replaced it.' She looked pointedly at Arx. 'Without my permission, I should add.'

'Impressive engineering,' remarked Molly. 'How does it feel?'

'It feels just like my old hand. I don't like it. I don't like the way it looks.'

Molly blew out smoke.

'You've certainly had your fair share of adventures.' Molly observed. 'Ed tells me you have a device implanted in your back too. You're carrying a lot of tech around with you!'

Cara grimaced.

'Yeah, well, not from choice, I assure you.'

She inhaled from her cigarette.

'So, what happens now? What does Ed want with me?'

Chapter 14

Of course, Cara didn't like it. She had reached her limit of invasive procedures from both humans and machines, poking around where they didn't belong. However, the Entity insisted, clarifying that it was a condition if she wanted to be allowed to continue her journey to find Mei Xing.

'If your so called 'Ed' is so powerful, why can't he transport me to Mei's world right now?' she complained.

'He could,' admitted Molly. 'But he won't.'

'I knew it! The bastard! He just wants me to suffer!'

Molly gave a thin smile.

'I think it's rather that he doesn't want to interfere and wants to allow you to find your own way.'

'That's not fair! I bet he knows where Mei is.'

'Probably,' agreed Molly.

Cara closed her eyes, her expression pained.

'I don't have a choice, do I?'

Molly just shook her head slowly.

A fully recovered and healthy-looking Cheryl had been transported into the tiny orange walled cell a few moments ago, much to the delight of Cara.

'At least it's letting us go,' Cheryl pointed out. 'It could be a lot worse. We could be prisoners.'

'For fuck's sake! I don't like being prodded and poked, being treated like an object. It feels like wherever I go, someone or something has to interfere with me. I would like to be left alone for a change!'

Cheryl put an arm around Cara's shoulders, trying to comfort her, knowing that for Cara, this was a big decision, but also knowing that if she didn't agree, they would be condemned to a life in this tower. The Entity had made it clear. If Cara didn't comply, then it wouldn't release them.

'I'd do it, you know I would, but it doesn't want me.'

Cara's shoulders slumped.

'I know you would, Cheryl.'

'Mechanical parts are more reliable than organic parts,' Arx stated.

'I didn't ask for your opinion,' Cara retorted. 'Obviously you're going to say that!'

'I do not understand your reticence regarding enhancements that improve your frail body. It is not logical.'

'Humans are not logical, Arx,' Cheryl informed him. 'You should know that by now.' She held up her hand when he started to reply.

'Now is not the time, Arx. You're not helping.'

Cara dropped her chin to her chest.

'I'm sorry Cara,' said Molly. She joined Cheryl and slid her arm around Cara's waist. 'There's nothing I can do. The Non'anan are emotionless and unfeeling. They don't understand us, which is why they want to study us. They're fascinated by how, what they consider being 'low order' beings can wield and direct the dark energy field. I'm pretty sure that they're worried about how we'll develop in the future.'

Cara sniffed, tipping her head to lean on Molly's shoulder.

'It won't hurt,' Molly continued stoking Cara's hair. 'If it makes you feel a little better, I've got one. Ed wants to keep tabs on me when I eventually go back home.'

Cara closed her eyes, sniffed once more, and sighed.

'Okay, I'll do it,' she whispered. 'If it means getting out of here and getting back on my way to be with Mei, it's a no brainer, really.'

Molly kissed the top of Cara's head. She released her arm and carefully stepped away, beckoning Cheryl to do the same, leaving a miserable-looking Cara sitting on the sleeping platform.

Watching her two friends move away, Cara, resigned to the situation, lay back on the platform. She didn't see Molly, Cheryl, and Arx disappear from the room, nor did she hear the accompanying crack of air. She was already unconscious.

With microscopic precision, the Entity delicately inserted a metallic disc at the base of Cara's skull. Once activated, thousands of nano fibres emerged. Over a period of an hour, the fibres grew, extending throughout her body like a network of intricate roots of a plant. They connected with organs and nerve clusters, creating a complex web within her body. Some connected with the semi-organic machine, implanted at the base of her spine, many more wormed their way throughout her brain, interfacing with key areas.

Cara was unaware of how extensive and invasive the procedure was. Once complete, the Entity would have complete access to every single aspect of Cara's being. Including her innermost thoughts, organ function, and even the levels of hormones in her blood.

The three women spent the next four days together.

Molly introduced them to her living quarters - designed by her and created by Ed, the Entity, for her three-year stay. They were quite expansive and luxurious, with a large kitchen diner and a bedroom with ensuite facilities for each of them.

Cara practically ran into her bathroom, shedding her dirty and smelly clothes to immersive herself in a deep bath, where she lay for a full hour, relishing the feel of the hot soapy water on her skin. She washed away the sweat and grime and for the first time in days, could wash her hair. When she finally emerged from the bathroom, she was pleasantly surprised to find that Molly had stocked a wardrobe and drawers with clothes. Not all were to her taste, but they were new, clean, and fresh. A sense of gratitude washed over her for this welcoming gesture, making her feel at home in this unfamiliar place.

It had been a long time since Cara had slept in a proper bed and she took full advantage. Each night, she would lie in sumptuous comfort with the soft sheets pulled up to her chin. She would call Mei and describe everything that had happened throughout the day. While Mei couldn't help feeling envious of the fun Cara was having with Molly and Cheryl, she was relieved to know that Cara was safe. They would talk well into the early hours of the morning, often ending their conversations making love, with Cara rising late each morning.

During the day, they drank real coffee and ate meals prepared by Molly, who turned out to be an excellent cook.

Time flew by as they shared stories, jokes, and deep conversations, basking in the warm glow of their friendship.

Until their final evening.

Molly couldn't conceal her sadness as they spent their last moments together.

'I'm going to miss both of you,' she murmured. 'It's been so nice having someone to talk to after being alone for so long.' Her demeanour shifted; her usual cheerful and bubbly personality was now replaced with sorrow. Eyes, once bright and lively, were now downcast. The atmosphere changed, casting a shadow over the once cheerful room that only yesterday was full of laughter and joy.

Cara grasped Molly's hand and squeezed.

'It's been wonderful, and I sort of wish I could stay here with you, but I can't.'

Molly gave Cara a sad smile.

'I know, you have to go, but I'm not looking forward to being on my own again. I'd forgotten what it was like to be with people.'

'Could you get Ed to bring someone to stay with you?' asked Cheryl.

Molly shook her head sadly.

'I've asked many times, but he won't.'

Cheryl hesitated. She looked from Molly to Cara and then back to Molly.

'I could.' she hesitated, licking her lips. 'I could stay here with you.'

Cara shot Cheryl a quick glance. Cheryl's offer surprised her. It hadn't occurred to her that Cheryl would be so selfless.

'I'm afraid that won't work, either. Ed says that the two of you don't belong in this universe. There are duplicates of each of you back on Earth. Which means that you can't stay here. I confess that I don't understand the implications of travelling between worlds, but Ed is insistent. You two have to go.'

'How about you coming with us?' asked Cara.

Moly shook her head.

'I volunteered for this. I can't renege on our agreement. I have to stay here for another year. I have no choice.'

The room fell silent as all three digested what Molly had just said. Then Cara quickly pulled Molly into a hug and squeezed her tightly.

'I'm so sorry,' Cara mumbled into Molly's red hair. 'I wish there was something I could do.'

'It's okay,' Molly replied, throwing her arms around Cara, returning the embrace. 'It's something I have to do by myself. I'll get through it. I appreciate you trying to help.'

'So,' Cheryl spoke up. 'We leave tomorrow morning.' She sighed. 'How about we forget about it for now and make this an evening to remember? Do you have any more of that wine?'

Molly grinned, disengaged herself from Cara, and made her way to the kitchen.

'You bet,' she called over her shoulder.

Chapter 15

In the morning, Cara had one of the worst hangovers she had ever experienced. She dressed in a new pair of jeans and T-shirt matched with a brand-new pair of hiking boots and exited her bedroom.

Molly and Cheryl seemed to have suffered no ill effects from the previous evening of excess.

'How come you two are so bright and cheerful?' complained Cara. 'My head is killing me.'

'Our Assists allow us to control pain,' explained Cheryl, her forehead creasing in sympathy. 'I'll get you a glass of water.' She strode over to the kitchen.

'Arx?' asked Molly.

'I can facilitate the removal of Cara's discomfort if she wishes,' answered Arx.

Cara sat heavily on the sofa, cradling her head in her hands. When Cheryl returned, Cara gratefully accepted the proffered the glass of water and downed it in one. Wiping her mouth with the back of her hand, she shot a glare at Arx.

'Using that machine, you put inside me, I suppose?' she growled.

'You did not complain when I removed your pain when you first awoke in this facility,' Arx pointed out. 'The device is there for your protection. It has saved your life many times over.'

Cara huffed. She couldn't deny that without it, she might be dead, but she still didn't like the fact that it had been implanted, even though she implicitly told the machines that she didn't want it.

'Oh, alright!' she blurted. 'Please do something about this hangover!'

Arx moved to one side and then back again.

The pain slowly faded until it was completely gone.

'Future excessive consumption of wine is not recommended,' said Arx. 'It has a detrimental effect on your fragile organic systems.'

Cheryl laughed.

'We know that Arx, but wine has some positive effects, too.'

'I cannot understand what the positive effects are,' replied Arx. 'Based on my observations last night, all three of you seemed to lose coordination of your limbs, at times your audio output exceeded the tolerances for the human hearing system and many times you were unable to control respiratory systems releasing strange noises and causing obvious pain in your abdomen.'

'It's called laughter,' replied Cara.

'I have no experience of laughter. I do not recommend that you indulge in this practice again.'

At this, all three women laughed. Arx, in his usual fashion, slid to one side and then back again.

'I've taken the liberty of re-equipping you both,' Molly said after the laughter had died. 'I got Ed to make some new clothes and camping gear. It's all in these new packs.' She indicated two backpacks on the dining table. 'Cheryl, I didn't touch your weapons.'

Cheryl thanked Molly and strode off towards her room to collect them.

Cara stood and embraced Molly.

'Thank you. You've been wonderful. I'm sorry we have to go, but I'm really glad I've met you. I hope the year flies by, and you can be back home soon.'

Molly smiled sadly.

'I can't tell you how much the two of you have helped me. I've been so lonely, but now I think I have enough strength to endure the final year. You're amazing Cara. I'm sure that you'll find Mei Xing wherever she is.'

Cheryl returned carrying a pistol and her Heckler and Koch MP5, which she stuffed into her backpack. She strapped a belt around her middle, checked the safety on the pistol, and slid it home into its holster.

Cara kissed Molly on the cheek and stepped back from their embrace. At the table, she picked up her pack.

'Is Mr Mapper in here?' she asked Arx.

'The non-functioning single node is in your carrying device.'

Cheryl strapped her pack on her back and walked up to Molly, taking both her hands in hers.

'Thanks for fixing me up, and thanks for being great company. Last night was really something!' She grinned. 'We certainly drank Cara under the table!'

Molly grinned back.

'We did. And her singing has to be heard to be believed!'

'Hey you two! So, I'm not a professional. At least I gave it a go!'

'And what about her dancing?' asked Cheryl.

Molly rolled her eyes.

'Is that what it's called? I thought she was having a fit!'

The two women couldn't contain themselves, laughing loudly, much to the consternation of Cara.

'Well, thanks very much!' she complained. 'When you've finished taking the piss, shall we get on?'

Molly's mood changed abruptly, a wave of sorrow washing over her. This was the moment she had been dreading - the departure of Cheryl and Cara, leaving her alone once more. She drew in a deep breath.

'I guess this is it. I wish you well on your journey. Maybe we'll meet again one day. I hope we do.'

Cara and Cheryl stood in the middle of the room while Arx floated over.

'So, how do we do this? Is Ed going to make a portal?' asked Cara.

Molly shook her head.

'He'll transport you directly. He doesn't need portals.'

'Oh. Where is he transporting us?'

'Somewhere you know,' Molly replied, a single tear running down her cheek. 'Goodbye, and good luck.'

'Do it Ed,' she projected a thought.

Cheryl, Cara, and Arx disappeared.

'INTERACTION BETWEEN HUMANS RECORDED.'

'Not so loud, I keep telling you. It hurts!' Molly winced.

'Is subject unaware?'

Molly sighed, wiping her tears away.

'Yes, she doesn't know. I still think we should have told her.'

'Observation requires normal behaviour.'

'I know that's what you want, but it's not ethical.'

'Ethics unimportant. Observation imperative.'

Chapter 16

'We're in the empty world!' shouted Cara gleefully. She turned to Cheryl. 'This is the world I first travelled to. The Machines have a portal from their world to here. We can get Mr Mapper repaired!'

But then, as she looked around, she noticed something strange, and the smile fell from her lips.

'Arx, why aren't the machines moving?' she asked, puzzled.

They had materialised next to the large tunnel that descended into the ground at a steep angle. Cara remembered it from her previous visit with Arx when he and Mr Mapper had created a portal from her cell in the Machine world. They had come here so she could get some things and to allow Mr Mapper to use it as one of the six mapping points to Mei's world.

But now, the procession of machines descending and ascending from the tunnel were silent and unmoving. The overly bright sun glinting from their silver, grey and black surfaces.

As she turned to survey her surroundings, Cara's eyes widened at the sight of yet more machines scattered about in various sizes and shapes. They stood still, their presence imposing, the silence eerie.

'What is this place?' asked Cheryl, her hand on her pistol grip still in its holster.

A gentle breeze blew Cara's hair. Birds chirped and called. The remains of the wood beyond the tunnel opening slowly swayed, their leaves rustling. There was no other movement.

On her right, the giant black disc of the portal to the Machine world stood large and looming. No machines were entering or exiting.

What had happened? The last time she had been here, it had been bustling with life. The machines were like ants, busily moving to and fro, some fast, others slow, a never-ending procession into and out of the tunnel, all on some unknowable mission.

Suddenly, there was a strange noise behind her.

'Eeek!'

Arx shot past her at breakneck speed, racing at the portal and disappearing into the black disc. In less than a second, he was gone.

'What's up with him?' asked Cheryl.

Cara's mind began to grasp what had happened.

'They're gone,' she said under her breath. 'They're all dead.'

Afterward

I hope you have enjoyed reading this book as much as I enjoyed writing it. If possible, please consider leaving a review on Amazon. Reviews greatly assist me in selling more books.

Thank you for taking the time to read my work.

Stay in touch with the latest news by joining my Facebook group: Search for "psi war", select Sci-Fi Novels (Psi War).

Visit: http://www.twauthor.com
Email me at: psiwarbook@gmail.com

Other novels and short stories available now:

Awakening: Psi War Book 1
Worlds: Psi War Book 2
The Cara Files: File 1 - The Chase
The Cara Files: File 2 - Automata
The Cara Files: File 3 – Starship
Echoes in the Static – A collection of short stories
The Bekkatron
The Ghost Hunter

Coming soon:

Together: Psi War Book 3
The Cara Files: File 5 – The Dead World
The Foe – A Maisie & Amara Adventure

Printed in Great Britain
by Amazon